playing with
Danger

OTHER TITLES BY JOYA RYAN

Desire Bay Series
Playing with Trouble

Captured Series
Break Me Slowly
Possess Me Slowly
Capture Me Slowly

Chasing Love Series
Chasing Trouble
Chasing Temptation
Chasing Desire
Chasing Mr. Wrong

Search and Seduce Series
Tell Me You Need Me
Tell Me You Crave Me
Tell Me You Want Me

Serve Series
Rules of Seduction

Reign Series
Yours Tonight
Yours Completely
Yours Forever

Sweet Torment Series
Only You
Breathe You In

Sweet Hill Series
Sweet Hill Homecoming
Sweet Hill Temptation

Hot Addiction Series
Crave

playing with *Danger*

A DESIRE BAY NOVEL

JOYA RYAN

Montlake Romance

This is a work of fiction. Names, characters, organizations, places, events, and incidents are either products of the author's imagination or are used fictitiously.

Text copyright © 2017 Joya Ryan
All rights reserved.

No part of this book may be reproduced, or stored in a retrieval system, or transmitted in any form or by any means, electronic, mechanical, photocopying, recording, or otherwise, without express written permission of the publisher.

Published by Montlake Romance, Seattle

www.apub.com

Amazon, the Amazon logo, and Montlake Romance are trademarks of Amazon.com, Inc., or its affiliates.

ISBN-13: 9781542048224
ISBN-10: 1542048222

Cover design by Letitia Hasser

To Mom and Dad,
All the trips to the Oregon coast for softball let me envision this entire town. Thank you for your support and endless memories.

Chapter One

Hannah closed her eyes and tried to drown out the low sounds of the bar she was currently tending. These tension headaches were getting worse and were now starting in her neck. As if she needed another pain in the neck.

Placing her hands on the glossy wood bar top, she slowly bent her neck to the left, bringing her ear to the top of her shoulder. Her black hair swayed across her back, and she made a mental note—she needed a trim before the jokes about looking like the local Morticia Addams started in from the regulars.

Pop!

She exhaled and rubbed her nape. Damn, she was stressed. And it wasn't just her neck popping—it was her brain.

The smells of beer and sea air drifting in off the surf just outside made for another typical Friday afternoon. She opened her eyes and got back to work. Though it was slow for midday, it'd pick up when everyone started to get off work for happy hour. She was working alone, as usual, and was the main bartender slinging drinks for this place. Sixty-hour workweeks, and she loved it. It was Goonies. A staple in town. The bar in town. *Her* bar in town.

Well . . . not exactly *hers* . . . yet.

"Hey, Hannah, my mug is dry," said Larry, a regular customer, pointing to his beer.

"Yeah, like your liver," Hannah said back. "You know, cirrhosis isn't sexy, Larry."

Larry rolled his eyes and just tapped his empty glass. The guy was a local, and Hannah knew him all too well. But she really couldn't talk, since she was as local as they came—and the only female bartender in the small town of Yachats, Oregon.

"The older you get, the meaner you get," Larry said.

Hannah scoffed while filling his glass. "That coming from Father Time?"

The man laughed and stroked his long, white beard. She'd known Larry since she was a kid. He'd worked with her father on a fishing boat out of Newport Bay, another town over. She'd learned quickly that all fishermen knew one another and were all blunt and dirty, in one way or another.

But being raised by an alcoholic fisherman who spent more time in jail than being her parent left for a tricky upbringing. Hannah relied on no one. That was one lesson dear ol' Daddy had taught her. Indirectly as it might have been. And Hannah wasn't about to argue her "mean" reputation. That was better than some of the other adjectives used to describe her around the town she'd called home since birth. Over the years, she'd heard everything from "trash" to "bitch" to "crazy." All of which she'd take over "pitiful." No, she'd never be pitiful. No matter how many times she'd had to bail her father out or beg Nancy down at the power company not to turn off the lights to their trailer.

That pain in her neck was starting to hum again.

She slid the glass toward Larry, and he just grumbled and took it, fusing his eyes back to the TV fastened above the massive shark teeth on the wall. The wood floors were original to the nearly hundred-year-old building and creaked with every hard wind gust the tides threw around. And when it was slow, Hannah could pick up the faint smell of saltwater taffy being made just one block down. Great thing about being located on Main Street in Yachats—it smelled like the ocean and candy 24-7.

She wiped down the counter, and when she saw Phil, the geriatric crabber, taking an extra-long look at her chest, Hannah made another mental note to remember not to bend over as much while wearing that tank top.

But if she wanted this place, she'd take it, and all the customers that came with it. Her boss, the owner, was looking to sell, and Hannah was ready to buy. The place made good money, and she could finally have something for herself. Outright and owned. She just had to get Mr. Bangs on board. He'd said he'd give her first opportunity to buy the place, and with her entire life savings, she thought she could convince the bank that she was a worth a small business loan for the rest. She just needed details from Mr. Bangs. Problem was, he never bothered to show up, really, or do much of anything when it came to the bar. Which was why Hannah pretty much ran the place already.

"You ever wear lipstick?" Phil said between the eight teeth he had left in his mouth.

"Excuse me?" Hannah said.

"Just asking if you wear lipstick. Would make you look real pretty."

She rolled her eyes. If Phil wasn't as old as the damn ocean, she'd smack him. Instead, she smiled her lipstick-free smile and said, "Nope."

The word *pretty* hung in the air, though. Very rarely had she ever felt pretty. Much less looked it. She was always working and always in some kind of ripped denim and tank top. Her hair was black and her eyes were blue—two qualities she'd inherited from her father—and she chose not to draw attention to either with makeup or products. She didn't need a reminder of whom she came from. She tried to outrun that fact every day, and to do so she looked in the mirror as little as possible.

"One of them tough girls. What do they call those?" Phil mumbled to himself.

But Larry chimed in from two seats away. "Tomboy. She's a tomboy."

"Well, glad one of us in this joint is some kind of boy, because between the two of you, you're pushing three hundred years old."

Larry just shook his head, and Phil laughed.

Hannah smiled and lined up the liquor bottles along the mirrored wall behind the bar. She might have tough skin, and people in town might think her rough around the edges, but there was a lot more to her.

She'd risen above enough to get respect from the majority of the townspeople. If not a little fear. Which was something she could deal with.

The bar phone rang.

"Goonies Bar." Hannah waited, and the voice was instantly recognizable.

"Hey, Hannah, it's Gabe."

Hannah took a long breath. Gabe Cleary, aka Deputy Gabe Cleary. Aka the same Gabe Cleary she'd gone to grade school with, who now was the law of the town. She instantly knew what the call was about before he said the words she'd heard a hundred times over the past several years.

"I've got your father here," he said.

"What is it this time?" Hannah asked, hoping it was just a drunk-and-disorderly and not something more serious, like a DUI or an assault.

"Intoxicated in public."

Thank God.

"He's sleeping it off in the drunk tank. You can come get him if you want, but he's welcome to stay until morning."

Stay in the cell? Wouldn't be the first time. Yet Hannah always went running to clean up her dad's messes. But she couldn't leave the bar, and she had no desire to go get him when he was passed out wasted. He was safe in the cell for now.

"I'll swing by after I close up the bar tonight," she said. That mental list of hers was getting longer, and the pain in her neck throbbed harder.

"No problem. He's the only one here, so he has the cell bed to himself."

"Ooh, the local jail cell is going to get a five-star rating this week."

Gabe laughed. "We serve, protect, and accommodate when we can."

Hannah smiled, but her chest was hollow. Deep down, she knew a big reason she'd never leave Yachats was because she had to make sure her dad was okay. He was little more than useless, but he was her dad. The only family she had. And she didn't want him to die or to hurt others. Since her mom had left when she was five, there had always been a sadness surrounding him, and Hannah could never break ties with him. It didn't make it right or okay. Made it fucking pathetic, and she kind of hated herself for it. But she couldn't leave him.

Maybe that's why she worked so hard to make herself untouchable. Maybe she'd think about that later. Or never. Because the minute someone started touching . . .

She shook her head. Something she'd done more in the last several months, every time that sunshine and warmth she'd felt once in her life started creeping in to remind her of a happy moment.

She hung up with Gabe and looked around. The bar was getting ready to pick up, Friday day turning into Friday night. And that's what she'd focus on. What she always focused on. Perfecting her untouchable persona and taking care of her bar. Yes. It would be *her* bar. Any day now.

She bent behind the counter just as she heard the door open and slam shut. A constant flow of people coming in was good for business. Which was why she was searching her lower cabinet for the reserve Jack Daniel's to put on the shelf.

"Excuse me?" a sexy, husky voice asked from behind her. "I'm looking for someone."

Hannah shook her head and didn't bother turning around. Still squatting and reaching back behind the vodka, she finally found the Jack Daniel's.

"Well, good luck with your search. Anyone you see in here is what you get."

She stood with the bottle in hand.

"I sure hope that's true," the sexy voice replied, "because I'm looking for my wife."

His words cut the air and hit her entire body like a blow, causing her hand to slip. The bottle dropped and shattered on the floor.

She turned slowly and saw him.

Him.

The one man she'd tried to forget over the past six months. The one man who'd ever gotten close enough to make her feel like more than trash. The one man who'd gotten her to say *I do*.

"Grant Laythem," she whispered.

His eyes were fastened to her face. Those same green eyes she remembered—clearer than the ocean she'd fallen in love with him on.

He smiled, but there was something very dark behind it. "Hello, Mrs. Laythem."

Hannah's skin flushed hot, and she felt the instant need to run . . . she just couldn't decide if the direction was away—or straight into his arms.

∽

Grant had always thought God to be the cold, vengeful kind. But when he stood there, faced with his wife, her beauty about knocked him on his ass. And for the first time in a long time, Grant thought God was throwing him a bone. Or a flare of torture, because while he was finally standing face-to-face with the woman who'd stolen his heart then sneaked off in the middle of the night with it, he couldn't touch her.

She was right there. Right in front of him.

And he. Couldn't. Touch her.

"How are you here?" she asked, a slight shake in her voice.

"Airplane."

She rolled her eyes.

"I mean, how did you find me? It's been six months."

He took a step closer. Though there was a bar between them, the rage and angst and general "missing the fuck out of this woman" was starting to boil.

"It's been six months, thirteen days, and three hours. East Coast time, of course."

She frowned. "You have it down to the hour?"

"Hard to forget the hour you left me on a damn boat."

"Please. It was a luxury cruise ship that docked in Florida. Not the sinking *Titanic*. I didn't leave you. Vacation was simply over."

A small smile tugged at his lips, but he wasn't happy. Not in the least. He'd almost forgotten how mouthy his wife was. And he liked it. It also made his muscles tick and his blood pump hot.

"Vacation or not, you left your husband and ran off. The redhead opted to go down with the ship for her man. You didn't even leave a note."

"And yet, you found me."

"I told you once that I'd always come for you."

Her lips parted, and her eyes skated over him. He didn't have to be a mind reader to know exactly what she was thinking. She was recalling the time he had come for her. The first time. All those months ago.

"Maybe I didn't want to be found?" she offered.

"Were you hiding?"

She bit her bottom lip. Something she did when she was nervous. He'd learned that over the two weeks they'd spent together.

"I don't hide," she said calmly, placing her hands on her hips and raising her chin.

He raised a brow at her challenge. So she had wanted him to find her. Otherwise she would have told him to fuck off by now.

That's when the truth hit him. So clear he could damn near read it off her face.

"You missed me," he said. Looking her up and down and watching those prefect breasts rise and fall on heavy breaths. "And you're happy to see me."

Pride swelled like a dry sponge dropped into water. Hannah's presence was hydrating, something he'd been missing more than he truly realized. His chest felt bigger, his lungs taking in more air, like he hadn't been able to take a deep breath in months.

He inhaled deeply, the empty cave that housed his heart finally feeling fuller. Warmer. Happier. He clutched at this feeling, because the next steps of his plan were going to be tedious and a pain in the ass. He'd need to recall this moment. Remember how it felt right now to breathe Hannah in. To know she was the only one who made him feel whole.

"I'm surprised," she said quickly.

"That's not a denial."

"Oh, I'm in denial, all right. Starting with what happened between us."

He adjusted the cuffs of his button-down shirt and flicked his wrist. His entire hand itching to land on all that creamy skin. Especially her bare arms and high cleavage.

Her thick, dark lashes against bright blue eyes made his hand itch more. Because he wanted to touch her face. See if her plump little mouth opened on a gasp when he kissed her. Like it had all those months ago. See if she remembered how much she liked kissing him. Because she did. He knew that for a fact. He couldn't get a single night's sleep without hearing her moans and soft pleas in his mind.

"Are you just going to stand there staring?" she asked.

His eyes narrowed, his whole face feeling stern. And judging by the goose bumps he watched break out over her skin, she felt his gaze, too.

"That's my right, isn't it? You being my woman, I can stare at you all I want."

She laughed. "Your woman? I don't know where you came from with that idea—"

"New York."

"—but I belong to no one."

"That's not what you were saying—pardon me, screaming—six months, thirteen days, and four hours ago. In fact, I'm certain you kept chanting, 'I'm yours, I'm yours, please, Grant, take me, I'm yours.'"

That made her bite her lip again, and she glanced around. Clearly assessing if anyone in the bar could hear their discussion.

Good.

He was getting to her, and he wondered if she could see how tightly wound he was for her. He hoped everyone heard him, because he wasn't keeping his wife—or what he wanted from her—a secret. And to answer her previous question, yes, he was going to stare. Because good Christ, his wife was more beautiful than he remembered. Granted, last time he'd seen her was technically on their wedding night on a cruise ship floating across the Caribbean.

He couldn't help but examine every inch of her he could see. Comparing it to the memory he had of her. Six months ago he'd enjoyed the sight of Hannah's sun-kissed skin in an itty-bitty bikini. He also knew exactly where she hid her tattoos. Now, he was staring her down in a dive bar in the middle of small-town Oregon, and she was in a black tank top and ripped jeans—all sexy badass. She looked harder. Tired. But still bright and gorgeous. Though he had a feeling she hadn't smiled in a while.

He couldn't help but stare, because it was then, being face-to-face with her after all these months, that he knew why he'd fallen in love with her so quickly. And married her even quicker.

"What are you doing here?" she asked in a low tone, taking a step closer to the bar that separated them. Grant didn't know if he imagined it, but he was pretty certain there was a longing in her eyes, and he hoped to God it was for him.

"I'm here for you," he said honestly. "And baby, you've been tough to find. Hiding or not."

She swallowed hard. He watched her throat work up and down. The busted glass on the floor crunched beneath her black boots as she slid just a little closer. She didn't seem too concerned with cleaning up the bottle she'd dropped.

"I didn't mean to surprise you," he offered, glancing at the mess on the floor.

"Yes, you did," she responded quickly in that snappy tone only she had. God, he missed that mouth. Especially when it was fiercely directed at him. Because the longer she mouthed off, the quicker her claws came out—and eventually those claws would be in his back while he was between her legs. Which was exactly where he intended to be by tonight.

"You're not unhappy to see me," he tried again. Rephrasing to see if she'd admit to wanting him. "Otherwise you would have told me to fuck off by now."

"Fuck off," she said quickly.

He grinned. Oh yeah, she missed him. And she'd be on him within the hour, at this rate. But she was keeping her voice low. Quiet, even. As if she didn't want anyone to know about him.

"Well, do you want to show me around town? Maybe introduce me to your friends, Mrs. Laythem?"

"Stop calling me that. And no. You should leave."

Oh, he could play this game, too. Fine, she was surprised to see him—he could give her that. But she was breathing hard and looking over his chest and mouth, and he knew what that look meant. She'd had it the first night he met her.

His vixen wife wanted him.

He just had to get her to admit it. Or drive her unease into irritation until she took out her aggression on him. Either way, it was a win for him.

"You know"—he leaned in, sticking his bottom lip out a little like a toddler would—"you keep whispering, and it makes me feel like you're ashamed of me. That hurts, baby."

She rolled her eyes again, and he grinned. Damn, he'd missed her. It had taken him only two weeks on a cruise he'd been suckered into going on by a friend in the first place to fall in love with her.

"Please. You're not hurt," she scoffed and crossed her arms beneath her incredible breasts. Which he would have appreciated more if her words hadn't just delivered a swift jab of pain and anger.

"You better understand one thing right now," he said quietly, placing his forearm on the bar. Keeping his eyes on hers, he said, "Don't you dare think that what you pulled didn't rip my heart out."

She blinked a few times, clearly surprised. Good. Because he might be Grant Laythem III, heir to Laythem Inc., a Fortune 500 company, and, as of recently, sole heir to the entire estate. But she didn't know that. Which was why he loved how she treated him. Like a man. A normal man. Some bum she'd met on a ship six months ago and fallen in love with, having no idea about his status or money or responsibilities of running his father's company in New York.

While she didn't need to know any of that, she did need to know that she had torn his fucking beating heart from his chest when she'd left him.

"It's been six months," she said softly, as if that explained away everything. Or perhaps she was asking him why it'd taken him six months to find her?

"Yes, it's been a long time. Like I said, you were hard to find. You don't have social media." And he had issues to deal with. Like when he'd woken up to find his wife gone and the ship docked, and he'd gotten a call from his lawyer saying his father was dying. That's right. His *lawyer* had called him. Vultures tended to circle whenever a powerful man with a lot of assets was fading. But all Grant felt was that it was his father in pain. And he'd wanted to be there. He'd had no choice but to get straight to New York. Then the last few months had been bogged down with going over his will and funeral arrangements and running the business, and yet, Grant still thought of Hannah every day. Life with her had been warm and sunny and easy. Sure, it had been short-lived, on a cruise ship in the middle of the Caribbean, but he missed it. She was the sun that relaxed him and the smile that fostered exceptional moments and steamy late nights. New York was cold and calculating, and he was always dealing with issues surrounding money. Always. But those were more details she didn't need to know about. He was here now. To get her to come back with him to New York as his wife. He just needed to convince her.

"Grant, I know things heated up between us quickly, but it was a two-week cruise, and it ended."

"Ended with us getting married. Who knew captains could wed people?"

"We both knew that," she said, deadpan.

"Exactly. Which is why I'm confused about why you're fighting this. You said yes. And baby, I'm here to cash in on those vows."

"Cash in?" She frowned, then looked around. "You can't have anything of mine. I was going to get the marriage annulled—I've just been busy."

Now it was his turn to frown. Grant was a fairly savvy businessman and knew when someone had a hand to lose. Hannah thought he'd meant he wanted money from her? Then she had looked around the bar.

Bingo!

"Is this your place?" he asked.

"No, not yet. No," she said quickly. Ah, there it was. His wife was a little entrepreneur. Looking to buy this bar. Okay, he could support that. Lot of money in the local joints. But he still needed her. So much. With his father gone, his mother still after the family fortune, and all of Grant's friends or former lovers after him for his status and money, he thought of Hannah, the only woman he'd ever opened up to. The only woman who'd loved him for him. She was brighter than the Mexican sun, and he needed her. His wife. In his world.

"I'm here for you. Nothing else," he said.

Her big, bright eyes met his. Creamy skin and dark hair that was so silky he could feel it just from memory. It was longer now. And that itch in his hand doubled. He needed to touch her soon, or he just might have to cut his damn hands off.

"What does that even mean?" she asked.

"It means I want *you*. Just like I did the moment I met you. Same as the moment you married me. I want you."

Her lips parted, and it made him think he had a chance.

"No."

Damn.

"Grant, we were crazy. We were caught up. We have two different lives. I'm sorry you came all this way, but I'll get annulment papers."

"Too late," he said. "We've been married over six months. It'd be a divorce."

She glanced away briefly, like his admission had caught her off guard. Which gave him another flare of hope. He had to test her, though, to make sure.

"So you must not have looked into divorcing or annulling the marriage?" he asked.

She glared. "I've been busy."

"Uh-huh. A two-second Google search is a big time commitment. Sounds like maybe you have no intention of leaving me. You wanted me to come for you and stay married." That sponge of pride started growing again.

"Whatever," she mumbled. "I'll get the papers drawn up soon."

He nodded and looked around. His mind was working double time to find a solution, because he couldn't lose her again. He needed a chance to make this work with her. He'd already lost his father. The one other person he cared about. Hannah was all he had left. The warmth in his cold, sterile world.

"So you won't even consider staying married?" he asked.

"There's no point, Grant."

"You don't want me?"

She looked him over. Same way she had the night they'd met. Same way she had these past fifteen minutes. It made his chest swell with pride. She looked at him like she was aching. On fire for him. And he wanted to be that fire for her.

"Me wanting you has nothing to do with it."

"That has everything to do with it."

"Lust, Grant. That's all it was."

He shrugged. "Agree to disagree. It was more. We both know it. So I'll tell you what—you give me a chance to remind you how good we are together."

She shook her head. "There's no point."

"Fine, then I'll get my lawyer to look over a divorce. Which means we'll split marital assets." He glanced around the bar. "This would mean I get to own half this bar of yours, right?"

Her eyes shot wide. "You wouldn't."

Her stance widened, her shoulders coming forward . . . his woman was pissed and in full attack mode. Or defense mode. Either way, she cared very much about this bar. Grant didn't exactly love himself for exploiting that. He loved *her*. And in that moment, it hit him how low he'd go to have another shot with her.

"I just want a chance," he said quietly.

"You're blackmailing me into being your wife? How sick are you?"

"Excuse me, you agreed to be my wife eagerly. I'm blackmailing you into *staying* my wife."

She huffed and shook her head. Grant wasn't above a little blackmail to get a few more moments with the love of his life. He'd never take her bar. In fact, he had a ton more to lose than she did. Which his lawyer and mother had made him very aware of. Thankfully, his mother didn't know he'd gotten married. But his lawyer did. Legally, he stood to lose a lot. Hannah could take Grant for quite a bit of his company, assets, and money. Which was why keeping his wealth to himself was wise for now. Once he could prove to her how much he loved her and they made this work, everything would fall into place—and sure, his lawyer had recommended getting Hannah to sign a postnup so that he wouldn't lose any of his company should they not work out. But he'd deal with that later. Mostly because he was certain Hannah would never drain him. He trusted her. He just didn't want to give her another complication to think about. He wanted her to accept him. Just. Him.

Because he'd already lost her once. Then lost his father. The only two people he ever genuinely cared about. And his father had believed in love. Said if Grant was lucky to find it, he should hold on to it. He wouldn't let his father down. Wouldn't let his company perish, and he would see to all his responsibilities *while* keeping his wife.

But one goal at a time.

He leaned in closer, placing both his hands on the bar, and felt her heat. She was two feet of wood countertop away from him. Her lips inches from his.

"Tell me right now that those two weeks we had together weren't some of the best of your life, and I will leave and give you your divorce right here and now."

Her eyes met his. But she said nothing.

"What do you want?" she whispered in a defeated tone.

"You. A chance to prove to you that we can work."

She closed her eyes. "We won't work. We don't."

"Give me two weeks." He figured he'd made her fall in love with him before in that time—he could do it again.

"Two weeks? Of what? Being your wife?"

"Yes," he said with a smile, liking the sound of that.

"And after those two weeks are up and you realize we don't work, you'll leave?"

He nodded. "I'll go, give you your divorce. Not taking anything from you. You have my word. I just want a chance."

She frowned. "Don't be thinking I'm just going to have sex with you."

"I think you'll want to." He winked.

"You're so annoying," she grumbled.

"And you're beautiful." He reached out his hand. "Do you accept my terms?"

She reluctantly took his hand to shake it. "Yes."

He cupped her small hand in his and brought it to his mouth to kiss her knuckles. Her flesh broke out in goose bumps again. Something he was getting fond of witnessing.

"That's my favorite word you say to me," he said.

"Well, don't get used to it." She snatched her hand away. "Now I have to get back to work and clean this mess up. So . . ." She made a "run along" motion with her fingers, and he rose to stand tall.

"Of course. Just point me in the direction of our home, and I'll be on my way."

"Our home?"

He nodded. "I'm staying with you, baby. Being married and all."

"Will you stop saying that?" she said quietly, looking around.

"Well, you can either tell me where we live, or I can hang out here with you and loudly yell sweet nothings about how our wedding was—"

"Four fifty-three Glenda Avenue," she said quickly.

He smiled. "I'll see you at home."

"Can't wait," she said sarcastically.

Grant walked out of the bar, feeling good for the first time in months. He had two weeks with his wife to convince her of forever.

He'd had worse deadlines.

Chapter Two

Hannah threw the door to the small Yachats Sheriff's Department open harder than she'd meant to. Thankfully, she'd gotten the rest of her shift covered so she could be there before midnight. It was just past eight and dark, but the station was still open, because the single cell had someone in it.

Her dad.

The light was on in the lobby. Which was two square yards of blue linoleum with a single chair next to a small table with year-old magazines on it.

"Hey, Hannah," Gabe said, getting up from his desk in the back. She could see the entire station from where she stood in the doorway. A small partition where Bette, the busty receptionist of sixty-five, sat during regular hours didn't hide the three desks and open area behind it. Because that's all it really took to run this small town. Nothing happened here. Except when the drunks in town didn't know when to stay out of town.

"Sorry about my dad," Hannah said. A line she'd uttered well over a million times over the past two decades. She adjusted her shoulders in her leather jacket. The squeak of the material sounded louder in the stillness of this office.

"Don't worry about it. I just brought him in. Kept it off the books."

"I appreciate that, Gabe."

Gabe nodded, walking around the partition and coming to face her. He was in his usual uniform. Badge and name tag shining brightly. Gabe had always been the good boy next door. Even dated Hannah's best friend back in high school. They'd been the quarterback and the homecoming queen, while Hannah was the weird Goth girl going through an angsty phase. Too bad no one had realized it wasn't a phase. It was her life. At eleven, she'd been scared all the time with worry for her dad. At fourteen she'd been annoyed by getting her dad out of whatever drunken jam he'd found himself in. At sixteen she'd gotten angry at him for the same old crap he pulled every week. At eighteen she went through a self-blaming stage, thinking she had ruined his life somehow and that's why he was the way he was. Finally, as a grown woman, she was just exhausted.

Twenty years of bailing her dad out.

Twenty years of disappointment.

And still . . . she showed up.

"Looks like I'm the real idiot," she mumbled to herself.

Gabe frowned. "What?"

She shook her head and gave her best fake smile. "Nothing. Long day. Talking to myself again."

"Like in math class," Gabe said with a grin. They'd been in the same classes most of high school, and yeah, she might have mumbled to herself through every algebra problem.

"Some things never change," she said and followed Gabe down the narrow hallway leading to the back of the office, then took a left down another hallway, where the walls went from a light beige color to gray. She knew the way. Had traveled these same steps countless times.

But still, she stayed behind Gabe, letting him lead.

They were still ten feet from the bars, and she could already smell her dad.

Wild Turkey and Marlboro Reds.

Ah, the smell of childhood.

She walked to the jail-cell bars and could feel the coldness radiating from the metal. She saw her father, lying on his side, one arm tucked under his head, sleeping on the thin cot in the cell.

"Where was he?" she asked Gabe, not taking her eyes from her father.

"Caused a fight at the Windy."

Hannah sighed. The Windy was a dive bar by the docks. Only fishermen and people looking for a two-dollar shot of whiskey went there.

"Did he hurt anyone?"

Gabe shook his head. "No, just pissed a few people off. He missed the guy's face and hit the wall, so his hand is scuffed up and swollen."

Served him right. Her father was a bad drunk. A fighter. He mouthed off and got himself into trouble, usually with guys bigger than him. A flash of cold goose bumps raced up her spine when she remembered her childhood stare downs with her father. He'd cocked his fist like a loaded gun on more than one occasion, but he never followed through. That was her blessing, she supposed. She actually felt grateful, because some kids had it way worse. Sure, he'd gone on tirades, but most of the time he just didn't care or show up. The fear of that fist coming at her was burned into her mind, though.

Could have been worse, she reminded herself. He could have connected that fist with her face. He never had. Yet the fear was still there.

"Sorry," Hannah said again, apologizing for her father. Who was snoring and didn't give a shit about anything but himself and his habit. One of these days he was going to get an assault charge. Thank God he hadn't tried driving.

"Silas," Gabe said softly, pulling out his keys to unlock the cell. "Silas, your daughter is here—"

"Hey, jackass!" Hannah yelled and kicked the bars with her boot. The clanging sound echoed and startled her father awake. "Get your butt up. I'm taking you home."

Silas Hastings grumbled and slurred his way to stand all his five feet seven inches of self into a swaying, upright position.

"That's no way to talk to me. I'm injured," he slurred.

Gabe got the door unlocked and slid it open. Hannah walked in. She just wanted to get his soaked ass back to his trailer and be done with him for the night. Until next time, that was.

"Injured?" Hannah crossed her arms, watching him steady himself on his feet. "You hurt your hand on a wall trying to punch someone, Si."

"Bastard cheated me!" Si yelled. "And I'm your father. How many times do I have to tell you to call me Dad?"

Hannah's fists tightened at her sides, then she immediately unclenched. Guess another thing she got from her *dad* was that jerky reaction.

"You tell me a lot, and I tell you no," Hannah said.

"You always were an ungrateful girl."

Hannah laughed. Honest to God laughed, because if she was ungrateful, she had no idea what to call Silas Hastings.

"Yep, that's me, Si. Spoiled and ungrateful. Now get your drunk ass in the car so I can take you home and make sure you don't choke on your own puke."

Si shook his head, agreeing with her idea and missing the sarcasm completely. Sarcastic or not, it was true. She'd take him home and put him on the couch in his trailer, with a bowl and a glass of water on the floor next to him. Just like she always did.

"Thanks, Gabe," she said to him as Silas made his way down the hallway, then slung his arm over Hannah's shoulder. She took his weight, helping him walk. It was the only time she touched her father. The only way she ever remembered him touching her. Never a hug, a high five, or a "way to go, kiddo" tap on the shoulder. Nope. It was always him slouching his weight on her, silently asking her to carry his load of baggage. Which was just as heavy as her father himself.

"You need help?" Gabe asked, keeping stride behind them.

"Nope, I've got this," Hannah said.

She walked her father out to her car, buckled him into the passenger seat.

"Good girl, Banana," Si mumbled, his eyes closed and his head leaning against the seat. Her heart lurched at the childhood nickname only her father used. Hannah Banana. "Love my little girl," he slurred. And Hannah didn't know if he was admitting to loving her or the little girl she'd once been. Either way, he mumbled things all the time when he was drunk. It was up to Hannah not to take anything to heart.

But that was the one part of her body that was aching.

Her heart.

Love you, Daddy.

She shook her head wildly, hating her brain for letting that thought sneak in. It hurt too badly to love a man like him.

She slammed the car door, walked around, and got in, making the quick drive to her father's trailer.

She almost forgot she had an entirely different man to deal with once she actually got to her own home.

～

Hannah stared down her front door and willed the night air to cool her skin. And her mind. Because both were racing hot, from a shitty night dropping her drooling and passed-out father off, to now having to deal with Grant Laythem on the other side of this damn door.

Was the universe trying to kick her ass with annoying males lately?

She'd specifically stopped her mind from taking a stroll down memory lane today. After Grant had come in, it had been difficult to think of anything but him. Yet she'd held strong. Refused to reminisce. Because the minute she did, she just might remember how good he felt against her.

"Snap the eff out of this," she muttered to herself. Twisting her neck from side to side, that throb always present, she blew out a heavy breath and tried not to replay one of the only things she'd been thinking about since seeing Grant today. Which was how hot he was and how hard up she was.

Grant had walked into her life looking polished, cool, and collected in his perfectly fitted blue suit, complete with a white button-down with the collar undone. She'd looked at the tan skin of his chest. Wondered if he still tasted salty, like the sea air, or maybe more like caramel.

She didn't know what he did for work, but she knew he was successful. She thought he'd mentioned some kind of business once. And she knew he was from New York. So he clearly had a posh life to some extent. Even the words he spoke dripped with poise and class. Even when he was being a brat or challenging her.

Yep, her ex was confident, and different from her in every way. He was also sexy as sin.

Scratch that.

He wasn't her ex.

He was her husband.

Her *current* husband.

Which she'd be taking care of really soon. Because despite her insane attraction to him, they could never work. Not long term. They were different, with different lives on different ends of the country.

She needed to focus on getting through the next couple of weeks, and that was it. In two weeks, everything could go back to normal. If she could just stop thinking about him. He was in her home, a single door separating them, and she knew it.

The lights were on in her small house, and it looked full and bright. Like his presence, even with her standing on the outside, was engulfing.

Out of sight, out of mind had worked for her the past six months. How bad could two weeks be with him hanging around just a bit? She'd walk in, ignore him, and go straight to bed. He was a dude, so he was likely passed out on the couch with Dorito stains on his shirt and *SportsCenter* on the TV.

Yep, just sneak by, and she wouldn't even have to acknowledge he was there. Good plan.

She opened the front door, set her purse down on the table, and kicked the door shut.

She got her coat off and heard a small clatter . . .

She looked up and saw Grant.

Shirtless.

A little sweaty.

And reaching high to the light fixture in the ceiling.

"Oh my God," she breathed, running her eyes down the length of his cut abs and tan skin. Her previous question was now answered: he definitely would taste the same. She could tell that just by looking at him. Paired with his chiseled chest and arms on full display, she couldn't help but fasten her gaze on the black leather belt that was making his crisp jeans ride a tad low. Enough to see where his happy trail disappeared . . .

"Honey, you're home," he said.

Hannah's eyes snapped up to meet his face, and he was smiling wide.

"And judging by the little bit of drool on your mouth, you must be hungry," he said. Knowing well and good she was just staring down at his package. Damn it. So much for avoiding him.

"You changed," she said. "I was just noticing you're not in city wear anymore. That's all." Good save. She gave herself a mental high five.

"Uh-huh. I own jeans."

"And what about shirts?"

"You don't like my chest? I thought it was your mouth that couldn't stay off it—"

"That was six months ago. Get over yourself," she said. Wanting to get *under* him. "What are you doing?" she asked, trying to focus on taking her boots off at the front door. Nice thing about her house was that it was small and open. Simple, one bedroom, with the living room and kitchen open and everything visible from the doorway.

Bad thing about her house was that now that Grant was in it, she could see everything, including his eight-pack abs, from about anywhere in the house.

"Just my husbandly duties." He smiled and reached back up to twist the light fixture again.

"Is that my screwdriver?" she asked.

"Yep," he said, his focus on the light. "This was loose, so I'm fixing it."

"I can do that," she insisted.

He glanced at her and smiled. "You're a bit petite to reach all the way up here, baby."

Hannah glanced down at herself. She was smaller but had curves. In no way tall by any means. Still, she was capable.

"Petite or not, I can handle myself."

"I'm aware," he said, the edge of his voice holding praise that caused a blush to threaten to creep up her cheeks. But she tamped it down.

"I also fixed the garbage disposal and adjusted the hot-water heater," he said.

She frowned, finally kicking her second boot off, and stomped in his direction.

"I don't need any of your help. I can take care of my home—"

"Our home—"

"And I've just been busy working, anyway. So don't bother. I don't need you." She didn't know if all her rage was pointed at him or the fact that she'd just had yet another run-in with her drunk father, or both. She just felt annoyed and crazy and . . . needy.

But she didn't need the way Grant was being useful. She wanted to claw at him, bite him, fuck him . . . she needed him in the way she remembered. The same way she'd needed him the night she met him.

And the two weeks following . . . He made her crazy in the worst—and best—ways, and now that he was here, she could use a dose of his brand of medicine.

She couldn't let her needs get in the way of the bigger picture. She *needed* to stay strong and get through these two weeks before her life could back to normal.

Is normal so great, though?

She shook her head, officially done with her brain. She closed the last inch between herself and Grant and reached for the screwdriver, but he held it out of reach and she tumbled into his hard chest. She instantly smelled his spicy skin and even tasted the hint of salt. Her mouth pressed against the upper set of his abs, and she instantly got wet.

And damn Grant for noticing. Because she felt his whole body turn on like a humming generator.

She backed away and looked him in the eyes.

"I was starting to forget what a tiny thing you are," he said, his voice huskier than it'd been a moment ago.

"Tiny and scrappy," she countered.

"Oh, I didn't forget scrappy," he said, lust tinting his words. "I still have scars on my back from those sharp nails of yours."

Her lips parted. She remembered the night she'd raked her nails down his skin. In fairness, she'd been so far gone to him and the passion that she hadn't realized. Also in her defense, he'd taken her like a wild man. On a secluded deck at 2:00 a.m., under the moonlight. She'd held on to him like her life had depended on it and dug her claws into his shoulders while the ship quietly plowed through the ocean in the dead of night.

"I don't remember you complaining," she said, trying to gain some ground.

He bent over her just enough to have his shadow engulf her. The yellow light haloed around him.

"And you never will," he said, shifting even closer toward her. "Because that was one of the best nights of my life." Closer. "I think about that moment every day. One of my favorite go-to memories."

She raised a brow, trying to keep her cool, but she wanted him closer. Just for a moment. Wanted to hear his words. His voice. Feel his heat. She wouldn't admit she missed him. She wouldn't even admit she wanted him. Even though every cell in her body was calling her a liar.

"Go-to memories?" she asked.

He nodded. "I've needed something to think about these past months to get me through this dry spell."

She eyes widened. "You . . . you haven't been with anyone since me?"

He frowned like she was crazy. "Of course not. We're married. Why, have you?"

She folded her lips. No, she hadn't. And she had thought of him. A lot. During that same dry spell he'd had.

"That's none of your business," she said.

He smiled. "So that's a no."

"How could you know that?"

"Because I know you, Hannah. Like it or not, I *do* know you. And I can tell you're faking calm right now. But you've missed me. So much that you haven't been with anyone else."

Her ribs crackled around her thundering heart. How in the hell could he guess that? No, not guess, *know* that. The bastard was so confident in his words that it made her whole body buzz like her skin was a neon sign flashing every secret and thought she had. She refused to give in, though.

"I admit nothing."

His grin widened, and he took another step until his chest was an inch from her mouth. "All right, then I'll admit everything," he said. "Starting with how those moans of yours are burned into my memory and every time I've come over the past six months, I hear them replay in my mind."

Her breath stalled.

"You thought of me?" she whispered. Knowing it was a dumb question, that it was opening the door for her to plant her mouth on him.

"Every time, baby. Only you." He tucked a lock of hair behind her ear and whispered, "I thought about fucking you from behind in front of the full-length mirror in your cabin. I thought about how all your sexy tattoos move and sway around your hips when you ride me." He trailed his fingers along her hips, as if outlining the vines and flowers she had etched there. "I thought about those little claws of yours and you screaming my name."

She couldn't breathe. Couldn't swallow. She could only feel him. Smell him. See him. He was invading every sense and bit of space she had. Just like last time. Just like that time they'd first met—and the two weeks that followed. There was something about Grant Laythem that got to her. A kind of power that went straight to her soul.

"Must have been a lot of lonely nights," she said, trying for any kind of cool and cursing her body for being so damn hot.

"And I plan to make up for every single one," he said. Leaning in, his mouth brushed hers. "Admit it, baby. You've thought of me." He gently grabbed her hand and brought her fingers between their lips and gently kissed her thumb. Then her middle finger. Then he bit her ring finger. "Tell me you've thought of me while touching yourself with these pretty hands."

She swallowed hard and thought back to every stupid time she'd replayed those two weeks in her mind. But she couldn't admit it. She also couldn't deny it.

"I think a lot of things," she whispered. Her resolve fading. It was hard to think with him touching her. "But I can't recall with you so close."

"For every memory you tell me, I'll take a step back," he bartered.

Deal. Because she needed space, or she was going to jump his bones right then and there.

"The ocean," she started. "When we docked the first time."

He smiled and made a motion to step back but waited for her to finish.

"I . . . we . . ."

"You pulled your bikini off and wrapped your legs around me," he said for her.

She nodded. "The water was up to our chests."

"You slid down on my cock, and the water moved around us."

"You fucked me hard," she finished, staring down the only man who made her feel weak and powerful at the same time. She couldn't hold out, didn't want to. She needed a release. Needed him. Just for a moment.

She grabbed his belt and yanked him back toward her, crashing her lips on his. The memory was too much. Grant being there was too much. She didn't need to reminisce—she needed to feel him. For real. Just once, to get him out of her system. Yes. That was why she was shoving her tongue down his throat. She'd avoid him tomorrow. Because he was right—he was her husband. Technically. And she'd never been so attracted to someone in her life.

"Jesus, I've missed you," he growled against her mouth.

She wanted to say she'd missed him, too. Instead, she just kissed him. Too afraid that the truth would come out if she didn't. Which was that this was short term. Crazy. Just like they were. But she'd give in for now. Because that's all she could do. Just give in.

She ran her hands up his chest, feeling all the hot, smooth skin and rigid muscles. She was desperate for him. Call it a dry spell or just plain hard up or that she missed him. Whatever it was, she needed Grant. He was the only one who'd ever sparked her blood like this. And right then, she didn't want to think of her situation. Didn't want to think of how the night had gone. Didn't want to stress and worry. She'd deal with the fallout and avoidance and getting through the rest of the two weeks later. Right now, she needed to douse the dry spell with some sexy man.

On her tiptoes, she wrapped her arms around him and clawed his back while she kissed down his neck and sucked on his chest. He felt familiar. Like she knew every square inch of his skin by memory and could draw a map with her tongue. Which she just might do . . .

She flicked her tongue out again, running over his pec, his nipple, and watching his strong heartbeat thump harder beneath the surface.

Clearly, he still loved her mouth on him.

"Oh God, baby." The low growl boosted her confidence. She still got to him. She could hear it, feel it, in how he cupped her head and his heart beat wildly under her mouth.

She sucked his nipple and lapped at his stomach muscles as her fingers dug into his back. She'd missed his taste. His skin. His strength. So much power under her fingertips right now, and she was bold. Wanting more. Wanting to feel alive. Wanting to slake all the pent-up lust and anger and everything on him.

She yanked open his belt and shoved his pants low on his hips.

His impressive cock sprang out, and she didn't waste a breath. She wanted to taste him. Feel him. Deep.

She hit her knees and sucked him hard. In one inhale, she took him deep into her throat.

"Fuck, baby. Oh God . . . yes."

She loved his sounds. Him weaving his fingers in her hair while she sucked him only spurred her on. A low growl broke from him. Like an animal. Wild and savage.

Before she realized what was happening, he had her up and bent over the couch. In one fast move, he pulled her pants down just enough to bare her to him.

"I've been waiting so long to feel you again, and the first time I come will be inside you."

With one big hand on her hip, he tilted her up and positioned his cock at her entrance.

"Tell me you want it," he said.

"You know I do," she said, looking over her shoulder at him.

His eyes were wild and fiery, like he would devour her. She loved it. He gathered her long hair in his hand and wrapped it once, twice, a third time around his fist.

"Then take it, baby," he whispered in her ear. With a tight grip on her hair, he surged deep.

She screamed his name but was met with the couch cushion catching her cries. He pulled out and hammered back inside her, using her hair as reins to pull her back while he surged forward.

He hit her in every spot, the way only he could.

She bit the cushion to stifle the cry of pure pleasure.

He was big and hard, and it had been a while, so he stretched her completely.

"Still hot and wet and tight for me," he said, pulling all the way out and thrusting back inside fast and deep. His open belt hit the back of her thigh, the cold metal gently clanking against her skin.

He unraveled her hair from his hand and gripped her hips. He was picking up speed. Thrusting in and out harder and faster. Every time he impaled her, he pulled her back. She knew he was making sure she felt every inch of him. And she did.

Her core slickened so much she felt every smooth glide of him piercing her, like he was made to be inside her. Such perfection couldn't be matched if she tried.

She bounced forward, the slap of his hips against her ass making her moan louder and louder.

"Say my name, baby."

"Grant," she said. "God, please, I'm right there."

"I feel you. You want to come for me?"

"Yes, yes, please."

He fucked her harder, faster still. She gripped the couch for support, letting her whole body go limp against the piece of furniture. She was at Grant's mercy, being held up by no power of her own, while he delivered slashes of pleasure into her.

He pulled her close, snaking one strong arm beneath her to lift her up so her back met his chest. His other arm wrapped around her waist, holding all her weight while he continued to pump in and out of her.

"I've missed you," he said against her ear, then bit the lobe just as his fingers found her core.

"Grant," she breathed.

His fingers found the sensitive bundle of nerves between her legs and rubbed.

"Say it again." His voice sounded more like a plea, and it made her want to respond. Give him anything he wanted.

"Grant." She said his name again and was rewarded with his magic fingers rubbing wet circles faster.

He thrust deep and stayed buried in her to the hilt.

With him inside her and his hand rubbing perfect friction, she couldn't hold out anymore. Her body melted. A tremor of heat raced from the base of her neck to the tip of her spine. She trembled, her body gently convulsing as she came hard around Grant.

"I love feeling you come on me," he said. His breath hit her neck, and she tried to speak but couldn't. Because just as her pleasure was tapering off, she felt Grant's hard cock twitch inside her and flood her with his own release.

He clung to her harder. Wrapping her in his strong arms as he came apart around her. But it was she who felt like she'd just shattered into a million pieces. And the only thing holding her together was Grant.

Chapter Three

"Whoa, whoa, whoa, back up. You're married?" Laura Baughman asked Hannah with big eyes. "I'm your best friend, and I'm just now hearing about this?"

Hannah slumped over her friend's kitchen table and rubbed her temple. She'd sneaked out of her own house this morning without a word to Grant. Who was still sleeping in her bed. His big, naked body looking all hard and delicious and . . .

That's when she'd hauled balls out of there.

It had been just past dawn, but thankfully, hiding at Laura's house came with complimentary coffee and a ton of questions.

"It was on the cruise I took last summer," Hannah admitted. Her one and only vacation. And it had ended with several voice mails that her father was in jail and her real life was calling her. When the ship had docked, everything had changed. Something she hadn't thought through then and didn't want to now.

"So now your hubby is back here looking for you?" Laura asked with a half-shocked, half-intrigued smile, and got up to get the coffeepot. She came back to the table and poured a warmer in Hannah's mug. Laura's light pink robe swayed around her legs, and her blonde hair was up in a messy ponytail. It reminded Hannah of when they'd had sleepovers in high school. Woke up early to talk about boys and gossip.

Only now, Hannah didn't need to gossip about boys—she needed to get rid of one.

Is that why he was in between your legs last night? Because you were so ready to get rid of him?

She cursed her own mind to shut up.

"Ugh, don't call him my hubby. And yes, he is back here looking for me. Well . . . he found me. So now he's just trying to convince me to stay married."

"That's romantic!" Laura said, her prom-queen optimism coming out.

Hannah scowled. "No, it's not. I got caught up six months ago, and I didn't think I'd see him again. So if anything, he's kind of stalkerish." Now Hannah was really grasping at straws, and judging by the look on Laura's face, she wasn't buying it, either.

"He's a man coming to see his wife. Because *you* married *him*," Laura said.

"Yeah," Hannah said, not taking her eyes off her coffee.

"On a cruise ship?"

"Yeah."

"In the Caribbean."

Hannah huffed an annoyed breath. "I get that you're counting facts, but we're not on *Sesame Street*. I made a mistake."

"Do you really think you made a mistake?" Laura asked.

"Of course I did. It was impulsive and dumb and . . ."

"And you've never done anything like that. Which means maybe he really is something special."

Hannah opened her mouth to say, "No fucking way is that possible," only nicer . . . but no words came. Laura's words were wiggling around in her brain, and the longer they stayed, the heavier they felt. Her temples pounded the word *special* over and over until it made her skull ache.

Special.

Grant is special.
What we have is special.

"No," Hannah said out loud, both to her friend and for her own peace of mind. Literally. "There's nothing special, and Laura, you're not helping. You're supposed to be on my side."

"I am. I just . . . maybe if you tell me how this even started?"

"What do you mean, how? We met, he was hot"—*still is*—"and I spent two weeks in a sex-induced lust coma cruising the ocean."

"Well, I'm going to need to hear all the details now!" Laura said, leaning over the table with excitement. "Start from the beginning. How did you meet?"

Hannah let out a loud breath and thought of the first time she'd met Grant Laythem . . .

"This has to be the reverse of what the *Titanic* going down felt like," Hannah mumbled to herself. She shoved the strap of her large woven bag up on her shoulder and followed the long line of people getting registered and onto the cruise ship.

It was her first—likely only—vacation.

She'd gotten the ticket from Roberta, an older woman back home who'd been planning to go on this Caribbean cruise as a single-woman getaway, but then she'd started dating, so she gave her ticket to Hannah. All she had to do was cover the flight from Oregon to Florida. Which was where the cruise started and stopped.

There Hannah was.

Single, alone, on a cruise ship.

Maybe she'd jump.

Or spend the whole two weeks drunk under a cabana. Either way, it was different from her small-town home with her small-town problems and even smaller-town reputation.

She was slowly shuffling with the large crowd to get onto the ship. She'd reached the first deck of staterooms when an announcement came on.

"Welcome aboard, passengers! I'm Captain Mike, and we'll be setting off soon. But while everyone is getting settled, the bars on all decks will be open, as will the pools and restaurants. So go have fun, and we'll get set to sea shortly!"

Bars were open? Perfect. It didn't matter that it was ten in the morning. Hannah was on West Coast time, which meant it was really 7:00 a.m., so a Bloody Mary sounded amazing.

She explored the top deck. Massive pools and hot tubs, all sectioned off with different themes. No kids' area. This cruise was meant for adults for sure.

So Hannah would be surrounded by retirees and honeymooners and single losers. Like her. But she'd make the best of it, since it was her one shot at sunshine and forgetting all the crap in her life. Like a dead-end job where she was starting to worry she'd only ever be a waitress instead of a business owner. And a father who was slowly killing himself with an addiction Hannah had been cleaning up after since she was a girl.

She took a deep breath of the humid air and found a small bar open and vacant. It was in the corner of the bow and had a Hawaiian tiki theme. She sat on the bar stool that was wrapped in fake grass and ordered a drink.

"Can I get a . . ." She should say something classy or normal for a morning drink. Like her go-to Bloody Mary, or even a mimosa. Instead she looked at the wall of liquor . . .

Fuck it.

"Three fingers of Gentleman Jack, please."

The bartender nodded. Didn't ask questions, didn't pass judgment, just poured her drink and set it in front of her.

"You look like you have the right idea," a husky voice said. Hannah looked to her left and saw the voice was attached to a sinfully sexy man with thick hair and piercing eyes. And judging by the white button-down shirt and blue slacks, he could use a vacation more than her. Though, in his defense, his clothes fit him perfectly. Expensive. She could almost see his toned muscles beneath the crisp cotton.

"Can I get the same thing the lady is having?" he asked the bartender. And again, the bartender silently poured and placed his drink in front of him.

Hannah took a sip of her own drink and tried to ignore the stranger.

But that was difficult, since he was looking right at her.

"Can I help you?" she said over her glass.

"I was just wondering who you were going to be these next two weeks."

"Excuse me?" she asked.

The man smiled, and holy hell, was it a smile. Bright, straight teeth, and his jawline was strong, housing the slightest dimples.

"You're on a boat for two weeks. Going to meet people, I'm sure." His gaze trailed over her, and she felt seen for the first time in . . . ever. At least, seen in a way she wanted to be seen. Because the beautiful stranger was looking at her like she was edible. And part of her really wanted to be eaten.

"You could be anyone," he finished.

Hannah nodded. "I suppose you're right." She watched him take a drink and lifted her chin in his direction. "Who are you going to be?"

He turned in his chair to face her fully. "Grant Laythem, only without all his problems."

She raised a brow. "Grant Laythem, huh? Sounds like there should be a 'the third' at the end of a name like that."

He laughed. "No, none of that. My mother wanted to torture me by giving me a name that sounded like a law firm."

Now Hannah laughed—and realized her drink was gone. Something Grant also noticed, because with a flick of his wrist, the bartender was back, filling both their glasses again.

"What kind of problems would a Grant Laythem have?" She looked him over. "Debutante balls and polo matches?"

"You think I'm a snobby rich guy."

Hannah took a swallow of her drink but kept her eyes on him. "Oh, I'm certain you are."

He matched her whiskey, only he finished his in one swallow, then rolled up the sleeves on his shirt. Hannah was transfixed by the action. Tan skin, strong hands, his forearms flexing with every inch that was uncovered.

"What if I told you I'm a regular guy?" he asked.

"Then I'd tell you I'm a regular girl."

"You're not?" Grant asked.

Hannah shook her head, noticing the alcohol making her brain heavy. "Just a small-town girl." A trashy small-town girl, but she'd leave that out. She'd follow Grant's lead and be Hannah, only without the problems. Like the fact that she'd spent her whole life trying to outrun the truth that she came from trash, and there was a big chance no one would ever see her as different.

She looked at Grant.

He was looking at her like she was different. He had no idea of her past, her father's past, any of it. And damn it, she'd give about anything to have a man like him continue to look at her the way he was.

But she needed to keep her strength. No way in hell was she going to get swept up in some white-collar guy.

"Tell me what a small-town girl like you thinks about," he asked.

"Small things," she said.

"No, I don't believe that for a second. I can see your brain working behind those eyes. You're a big-picture woman."

She bit the inside of her cheek to keep from telling him he was right. Instead, she lifted her chin in the air with all the confidence she could muster.

"Well, I can see where this big picture is going, and I can tell you right now, I don't need to go 'check out your room' with you, since I'm pretty sure they're all the same."

He smiled and leaned closer to her. "You think I'd come at you with a presumptuous line like that?"

"Maybe."

"Well, I wouldn't. I'd come right out and ask you if you wanted to come to my room—for inappropriate reasons only."

That piqued her interest. "Oh? And what kind of inappropriate reasons would those be?"

She'd meant that to sound playful, but her words were laced with curiosity and lust.

He rose from his seat and placed a bill on the counter for a tip. He then gripped the back of her bar stool and leaned in so close, she could feel his lips on her ear.

"Come find me tonight at the Red Bar on deck two, and I'll tell you every single reason."

She didn't answer him. Just felt his heat draw back as he walked away.

~

Everything was color-coded around here, right down to the bars. The Red Bar . . .

Hannah looked around and admired the bright blues surrounding the dark cruise ship bar. Not red. Nope, she'd decided that after her encounter with the mysterious Grant Laythem, she wouldn't be finding him.

Just their one encounter had left her hot twelve hours later. Now, drinking on a ship, surrounded by people, she felt the blue from the walls, the decor, sink into her bones.

Blue.

She glanced down at her simple dress and realized it was blue as well. Figured. It showed more cleavage than she ever had, mostly because she never wore dresses. But she'd bought this for the cruise, thinking it'd get her out of her comfort zone. It was tight, fit every curve, and she liked it.

She looked around, holding her drink in her hands. Surrounded by people, the loud music vibrating through her bones and humming down her spine.

She sipped her drink just as a man approached her. He was average height. Cute. Fit. For all the basic reasons, he was attractive.

But Hannah couldn't even think about getting hit on or putting in effort to whatever it was this guy was saying. Her brain was spinning around the idea of "basic reasons."

Instead . . . it wondered about Grant and his "inappropriate reasons."

"I'm Chuck," the guy said loudly over the music, snapping Hannah back to reality.

"Hannah," she said back.

"You are gorgeous," he said.

She nodded. "Thanks."

He started to say something, but Hannah jerked slightly when she felt a large hand rest on the small of her back.

She turned around to find Grant, staring daggers at her.

"Oh . . . is this your friend?" Chuck asked, looking at Grant and clearly wondering if he still had a shot with Hannah.

"No, we're not friends," Hannah said.

"No, definitely not friends," Grant agreed, his hand running just an inch lower. He leaned into her ear so only she could hear. "I really hope you're color-blind, baby, because I've been waiting for you."

She looked over her shoulder and met his eyes. "I never said I'd come."

He grinned, but there was something sinisterly sexy in his eyes. "Oh, you'll come."

Grant returned his attention to Chuck. "Excuse us." And that was all he said before leading Hannah to a dark, shadowed booth in the corner of the Blue Bar, where the music wasn't as loud and the people were all facing away from them.

"That was rude," Hannah said and sipped her drink, her body buzzing with warmth being near Grant again.

"You're right—that was rude to keep me waiting."

She frowned at him. "Clearly you found me."

"Because you enjoy being chased?" he asked. But before she could answer, he finished with, "Why didn't you meet me?" His voice was deep and insistent. He looked better, if possible, than earlier. With a fresh shirt and slacks, he looked classy, put together, and capable of anything. Something that had her imagination going.

"Why did you want me to?" she asked, turning the question back on him.

"Because there's something in your eyes . . ." He stared straight at her in that way only he could do and made her feel seen again. "That makes me drown."

"Drown in my eyes?" she asked, ready to knock away his lame line.

"Drown in the sadness behind them."

That made her breath hitch.

"This coming from a man that has his own brand of pain behind his eyes," she countered, trying not to get lost in the deep, dark pools. But he was hypnotic. And he might be a stranger, but she'd recognized his darkness right away. Because she felt it, too.

"You think I'm in pain?" he asked.

"I think there's more to you than you let anyone see."

"Why do you think that?"

"Because of how guarded you are, but you disguise it with bluntness."

Grant's lips parted slightly, and Hannah felt like she'd just seen a side of him that she would guess not many saw. A hint of honesty. Vulnerability. And she liked it. Wanted to know him more. To tap into that moment and follow it wherever it took her.

He cupped her neck, his thumb trailing along her throat, and she felt so small, so vulnerable to him. He brushed his lips overs hers, and when he spoke, his words hummed against her mouth.

"Come to my room with me," he said. Then he took her upper lip between his two. Kissing her intently, long enough to stroke his tongue inside, then he pulled back only to let her answer.

She tried to keep her composure.

"Come to your room, huh? What, to see the great view?"

She felt his smile against her lips. "You're a mouthy woman." He kissed her again, taking a deeper taste, the feel of his warm tongue inside her mouth making her eyes flutter and her whole body heat ten degrees in a single second. "And the only view I'll have is between these pretty thighs of yours."

His voice was raspy, and Hannah opened her eyes to see him looking at her. His hands on her. Waiting for her to give the go-ahead.

She couldn't deny this man, this Grant Laythem.

Because she had a feeling if she walked away now, she'd miss out on something she'd never have the chance to feel again . . .

Chapter Four

Grant shifted between dream and waking and, through the fog, wondered if last night had been real. He smiled, not opening his eyes because he felt the soft flannel sheets of the bed. Not his bed. His sheets were pressed and cold and back in a sterile penthouse apartment in New York. These sheets were warm and soft and well loved.

His wife's sheets.

His wife's bed.

His smile widened, knowing last night had been real, and he opened his eyes, hoping to be met with the sexy, warm body of his wife . . .

Empty.

He looked around the small room. The dresser had random jewelry, a sweater, and two coffee mugs on it. The little chair in the corner held a basket of clean laundry. And Hannah was nowhere to be found. The sun was shining through the window, and the slightest smell of ocean air wafted through the entire place.

He was in his wife's home, small town, and bed. And yet, he was alone.

"This will not do," he mumbled to himself. He missed her. After last night he was sure she missed him, too, and the rest of these two weeks would fly by. Because he remembered how quickly things had heated up between them the first time.

She was stubborn. She made him work for it. For her. And he liked that. The woman had refused to even meet him the first night on the ship. He'd had to go track her down, and even then, she'd pegged him. From moment one, she saw something deeper in him that no one else ever acknowledged. And from moment one, she was a pain in his ass. But he saw the sadness in her eyes. It was a match made in hell, on a ship, and the best thing to ever happen to him.

Because Hannah was everything. There wasn't just one moment that made him know that. It was all moments. Even down to the way she melted for him . . . depending on her mood. Oh, she always melted, but the level of aggression was always measured by her needs. Needs he loved fulfilling. Whether it was making love; hot, passionate sex; or full-on, dirty fucking. Whatever she was in the mood for, he'd do it all, because it was all good with her. And then he'd convince her to come to New York with him, and the rest would be history. Love and happiness for all.

Boom.

Done.

Good plan.

His cell phone rang from the bedside table, and he lunged to grab it.

"Grant Laythem," he answered, rubbing the sleep from his eyes and sitting up in bed.

"I've left two messages and stopped by your apartment yesterday. Where are on earth are you?" the familiar shrill voice barked from the other end of the line.

"Hello, Mother," he said. "I'm out of town." He made sure to leave out details, because while he was required to love his mother, he also wasn't blind to her motivations. Which were money. Particularly his late father's money.

"Well, we have a company to run. I need to discuss the logistics of your father's will, and your lawyer hasn't called me back."

"That's because he can't talk to you. Your lawyer needs to talk with him, and honestly, Mother, there's not much to talk about. Dad left everything to me. You two haven't been together in years."

"But we're not legally divorced. You know that," she said. Grant could almost hear her pearls shuffling around her neck.

And yes, he did know that. Though his parents had split up over ten years ago—due to his mother's infidelity—his father kept paying her expenses after their separation because he was a good man. And his mother took full advantage of that. Something she would not continue to do with him. No matter how big a fit she threw.

"I'm not going to discuss the company with you," he said. "I'll be back in New York soon."

"I'm your mother, and you're treating me like some common employee."

"No, I'm not at all. My employees show up and actually work for a salary."

"Oh, I put in my time with your father, and he knew his part in the separation. I'm still his wife. Now his widow. And that counts for something."

Not to Grant, it didn't. How could she be that entitled? She'd never cared about anyone's feelings but her own, and her top priority was money.

Grant closed his eyes and tried to think of one good thing about his mother. Just one.

She was always around for me growing up . . . nope, that's not true.
She taught me how to treat a woman . . . no, that's not true, either.
She loved me . . . no.

Grant was certain that his mother was only capable of loving herself. His father had been responsible for how he turned out. He tried every day to be the best man he could to make his father's memory proud. Because he owed everything to him.

His mother was the kind of woman Grant never wanted to know, and yet, he was surrounded by that kind of woman. Fake, ruthless, entitled. Which was why he'd fallen in love with Hannah so quickly and easily. The only commonality she had was the ruthlessness. But she used that for good instead of evil.

"The will stands, Mother," he said curtly.

"Don't you dare hang up on me," she said.

"Talk to your lawyer, and he'll talk to mine."

And he did hang up. Because he couldn't bear to deal with the woman who'd given him life, then sucked it out of him.

How could someone be so evil? She didn't love his father. Grant wasn't even convinced she loved him. His mother loved money. And Grant had to make sure that the one thing his father had left behind would stay intact. His company was all he had left of him. And Grant wouldn't let anything happen to it. Including having pieces sold off to his mother due to the technicality that she was now legally a widow.

He shook his head. The timing wasn't on his side. His phone buzzed again, and it was his lawyer. He sent it to voice mail. Surely his company wouldn't fall apart in the time he was gone. He still checked in. But his board only had one meeting later this month, and they weren't voting on anything life changing. Two weeks for him to take a breather to get his wife back was reasonable. He wouldn't let his mother get his father's company, and he wouldn't let anything go to ruin. He also needed to get Hannah on board in the two weeks he'd planned, because he couldn't take much longer than that away from the city or his responsibilities.

He got up out of the best rest he'd had in a long time and felt the sting of morning air hit the welts on his back. His wife was a feisty one, and he loved feeling her even though she was gone.

He walked out into the living area, which was small but homey, looking extra-long at the couch. He already loved that couch and had fond memories of his wife bent over it just last night. That would put a spring in any man's step.

He went to make a pot of coffee and saw a pink sticky note.

Left early for work. Don't be a bum today.

~H

He smiled at Hannah's flowy script. The woman worked hard. Or she was avoiding him. His money was on the latter. But she couldn't stay gone forever. He'd proven that. And there was no way he'd bum around when he had his woman's heart to re-win and plans to remind her how good they were together.

Judging by last night, his recall was sorely lacking, because she was better in every way than his poor excuse for a memory. She was wild and passionate, and he felt her love for him. Whether she admitted it or not. Just like he'd felt it six months ago. And that was what he'd remind her of. Because he'd had his share of cold women. Women who always had an agenda. Women who wanted something from him. Not Hannah. Never Hannah. She just wanted him. She also didn't know exactly what he could offer—like a fuck load of money—but that was best kept secret for now.

But he'd show her just how good having a husband around could be. Starting with a stroll into town.

~

Hannah dunked two martini glasses in the sanitizing solution behind the bar, then put them in the mini dishwasher. Then repeated the task with small tumblers. The owner clearly didn't give a crap about cleaning up after closing last night. Rudy Bangs was almost useless. Other than being a fairly nice guy and coming in for Hannah when she needed a break—like last night, so she could leave by dinnertime to go get her dad out of jail. But as an owner, or even a bartender, he sucked. Didn't do shit.

Which was why he was looking to sell and Hannah was looking to buy. If only he'd just commit to actually selling the bar instead of talking about it.

She kept washing dishes, taking advantage of the slow late-afternoon shift.

She thought about the sticky note she'd left for Grant this morning. Did he read it?

Was she mean for ducking out at 6:00 a.m. and hiding at Laura's house until now, when she hid at the bar? *Work*. She was working, not hiding. And she'd keep telling herself that until she believed it.

How had things gotten so complicated? How had she gone from single and miserable, to married on a cruise ship, to wife on the run, to wife for two weeks? Grant had a knack for complicating her life, but he also had a knack for making her happy.

And there she was, thinking of him.

Thinking about last night.

She wanted more already. She was forcing her brain to recall every detail, every touch, every move. She tried to remember the exact way it felt when he slid inside her the first time. How the couch cushion had scratched against her mouth when she screamed into it.

She wanted to relive every second over in slow motion.

And that was the problem with Grant. It was always better than good and over too soon.

"Is it always this dead in here this time of day?" Rudy said, walking through the front door, his big Santa Claus belly sticking out from his blue jeans and covered in a stained white T-shirt. He looked like he'd just rolled out of bed.

Hannah glanced around. "Yeah, this is pretty typical between lunch and happy hour," she said. Sure, Rudy covered for her now and again, but only when the other backup bartender wasn't able to work the part-time shift.

"Well, I'm glad you know," he said, coming to sit on the bar stool. Hannah knew his drink, and owner or boss or whatever he was to her, right now it was clear he was a customer, so she grabbed the gin and poured him a few fingers.

"I do know about this place, right down to the smelliest customer and tiniest crack in the floor."

Rudy nodded and took a sip. "Well, then I suppose you should own this place," he said.

Hannah almost dropped the glass she was holding. Her eyes darted to Rudy.

"What?" she asked, too scared to hope.

Rudy smiled. "You've been squawking for months that you want to buy this place. I'm selling, and I'm coming to you first," he said.

Hannah's mouth dropped open, and she lurched over the bar and hugged her boss.

"Whoa. Easy there, girl. You start handing out free hugs, and business will boom!" Rudy said, chuckling.

Hannah scooted back off the bar and stood, her heart racing in her neck.

"It's mine? It's really mine?" she asked, needing to hear once more that she was finally going to own Goonies Bar. Finally have a career, something of her own. Something she'd worked for.

"I know you've been wanting to buy this place for a while, and I promised you'd get first bid."

She wanted to hug him again, but Rudy continued before she could.

"There's just one catch," he said, and Hannah knew there always was. That happy heartbeat in her throat stilled while she watched Rudy's mouth, waiting on his every word.

He let out a breath. "The bank is set to foreclose on this place and put it up for auction unless I can pay off what I owe. Well . . . back owe."

Hannah's eyes went wide. "You never told me the bank was going to take the bar. And what do you mean, 'back owe'?"

"I haven't exactly paid on this place as well as I would have liked."

Hannah frowned. "This place makes great money. We come out in the black every year. Even in our slowest months we're still ahead."

Rudy nodded and took another drink. "Yeah, I know business is good. I just . . ."

Hannah knew the rest of that sentence without Rudy saying it. He had a gambling problem. And a being-lazy problem. Hannah wouldn't make him say it, but she knew it. She also knew this bar could be great under the right ownership. Which was why she wanted it so badly. She could do a good job. But if the bank got it and auctioned it, she didn't stand a chance at owning it. Highest bidder usually had cash—or more of it than Hannah had, at least.

It was her turn to let out a breath. "How much do you have to pay off?" Hannah asked.

"Twenty thousand in ten days."

"Jesus Christ, Rudy!" She looked around. Gus was three stools down and glanced her way. Hannah leaned closer to Rudy and lowered her voice. "Why didn't you tell me?"

"I thought I could handle it," he said. And it was that expression, that tone in his voice, that always got Hannah. The look and sound of sorrow. Rudy wasn't a bad guy—he was just bad at running a business. And she didn't want to see this place go under or into the hands of someone else. She didn't want to see Rudy go under, either.

But his "handling it" entailed him drinking and going to Seven Feathers casino two towns over, like he always did when he had a problem.

"Anyway, I know you're good for the loan and can get that through the bank," he said. "So you can still buy the place."

Yeah, that's because Hannah had gotten preapproved last month, when she and Rudy had started talking seriously about it.

"But there's going to be nothing for me to own if the bank takes it and auctions it."

"So pay them off first," Rudy said, like it was that easy.

"Rudy, I don't have twenty grand to bail you out, then to put money down for the loan."

He took another drink and sighed. "I'm sorry, Hannah, there's nothing I can do, then. If I don't pay, this place goes up for auction late next week."

There was no way she could outbid anyone. She was sensible, and getting a loan was already hard enough.

She only had fifteen thousand, and that was her life savings. She still needed five grand in ten days just to pay off the delinquent balance. Then she'd have nothing to put down. She'd have to hope the bank would finance the entire loan . . .

"I'll make it work," she said. She looked Rudy dead in the eyes and meant every word.

Rudy, however, looked ecstatic. He clapped his hands once. "Good girl! Then the bar is yours."

"I'll have the balloon payment by the due date. But I want the papers drawn up that this place is mine."

He nodded. "Deal's a deal."

She nodded and shook his hand. Now she had to get really creative about how to raise five grand in roughly a week.

As if she didn't have enough on her plate.

∽

So far Grant had taken his time getting ready and wandering around town today. Though he missed Hannah, he loved being among her things, in her town. He'd sat at her kitchen table and drunk coffee out of a mug he'd gotten out of her cupboard.

He felt closer to her. Anticipating that she was nearby, and that while he'd woken up without her this morning, she couldn't escape him. He would see her again. Tonight. And then the next night. And then the rest of his nights, forever.

"One step at a time," he said to himself, walking down Main Street.

He came up to a cute little home goods store that looked like it had a massive warehouse behind it. He looked the establishment over. The business was clearly working a hometown angle—he liked it.

He'd spent the last hour checking out the small coastal town and had learned that most of everything relevant was on Main Street and within walking distance. The entire town was modeled to look cute and clean, with the same curb appeal.

From the looks of—he read the sign on the store he stood in front of—Baughman Home Goods, this could be the perfect stop for a new screen door for Hannah. And there was a ton of flower displays in the front window. Getting her a bouquet of fresh flowers would be a husbandly thing to do. She could walk in after a long day, and he'd have them waiting for her.

Yes, that was the husband he'd be. One who appreciated his wife. One who wanted to show how much he thought of her. First, he just needed to get her to like him. Hence, the flowers.

He opened the front door of Baughman Home Goods and was greeted by a large man. Grant's height, but built like a tank. Not the kind of guy he'd expected to see running a flower shop. The kind of guy he'd expect to see running in the NFL.

"Hey, friend, how are you today?" the man asked with a genuine smile.

Grant read his shirt—the stitching spelled out "Jake." Looked like the guy worked there. Couldn't get service or kindness like this back in New York. Grant liked the guy already.

"Pretty good, just hoping to get a few things," Grant said.

Jake nodded. "Great. Well, let me know what I can help you with. We have everything from outdoor to indoor home repair and lawn care."

"Ha, good slogan," Grant said.

Jake frowned, as if replaying what he'd just said, then finally smiled. "I didn't even realize that! I should write that down. You in marketing from the city?"

From the way Jake looked Grant over, he could tell Grant was not local. Maybe he needed to ditch his slacks and button-downs. He mostly wore suits every day and just left the jacket off. But maybe he could take it down another notch.

"I'm just visiting. I'm in business, but marketing is a big part of it."

"That sounds cool," Jake said. "So you just consult with businesses?"

"I own my own business, and the main goal is under that umbrella. There's several small businesses."

"That's awesome," Jake said. "I own this place with my wife, Laura. That's her name on the sign out there. It's great having something of your own, isn't it?"

Grant thought of his father's business. Thought of how it had never really felt like Grant's. He'd inherited it, but he wanted to add to it. Wanted to contribute. Build on his own branch and make something of himself with the opportunity he was given.

"Yes, it is," he said to Jake. Curiosity got the better of him and he zeroed in on the one word Grant wanted to use himself: *wife*. "So you work with your wife?" he asked. Like discussing this matter with a nice sales guy made him part of this special husband club. A thought he enjoyed.

"Yep, I do." Grant could see the pride coming off Jake.

"How's that work out?"

"Great for us," Jake said. "You hear those horror stories about husbands and wives working together, and how one will end up killing the other." Jake leaned in and lowered his voice. "Honestly, in the beginning, I thought my sweet Laura might accidentally hit me over the head with a shovel, but those days are behind us." He straightened and smiled. "Plus, it would have been worth it just to watch her walk around in a skirt all day."

Grant laughed. Jake was a salt-of-the-earth kind of guy who loved his wife and had no trouble talking about it. He also liked hearing that marriage wasn't always sunshine and roses, so that added to his mental hope jar. Hope that he and Hannah would really be okay and work everything out.

"But you get me started talking about my wife, and I'll go all day. So what can I help you with, my friend?" Jake asked.

"Any chance you have screen doors?"

"Yes, that'll be back in the warehouse. I can show you."

Grant thanked him and followed him to the back. "So you're new in town?" Jake asked over his shoulder.

"I stand out that bad?" Grant asked, glancing down at his pressed navy slacks and white button-down shirt for the second time.

"Nah, I just grew up here. Locals know locals."

Grant nodded. Guy was nice. Was liking this local idea. Being from a city, there were cold, hurried people everywhere.

"How long have you and your wife owned this place?" Grant said, glancing around at the massive inventory and thinking that a business like this must make a killing. Had the market on the home goods, it looked like, for the entire town.

"Technically, not long. But I've worked here since I was a teenager and took over for my father-in-law. Lot of sweat equity. But my wife is the brilliance behind everything. Especially the flowers in the shop up front."

Grant nodded. Partly because he was starting to think he might have some investment opportunities around this place and could start to add to his father's holdings, building his own portfolio and getting his hands in some local business.

"This is a great place," Grant said. "All your product is local?"

"Absolutely," Jake said with clear pride. "No big chains or mass product from overseas. It's all done right here. My buddy is building the log cabin subdivision across town, and we supply him with the wood and landscape."

"That's incredible—you can all self-sustain and even thrive with this small dynamic."

"Thank you. Sounds like you really know your end of business," Jake said, rounding the home repair area of the warehouse and getting to what looked to be doors ahead.

Grant couldn't help his business mind. He was always looking to invest and grow the company by taking on new ventures. Especially ones he could take credit for as his own finds. He also loved funding small businesses, especially where there was profit to be made. That was what a conglomerate was for. To oversee the success of many smaller businesses.

"I'm in the business of making other businesses thrive," Grant said vaguely. But the way Jake spoke of his wife made Grant want to relate. "I'm also here to see my wife."

Grant didn't know why he'd said that. Maybe he wanted to continue this real conversation with a real person who didn't have a secret agenda like everyone back in New York. Maybe he wanted to brag about Hannah. Talk to someone, married man to married man. Because the truth was, he'd never had the chance to do that.

"Your wife?" Jake asked, showing him to the screen doors. "She local?"

"Yeah. Hannah Hastings."

Jake choked on what sounded like a shocked breath. Finally, the giant man gulped air and let out a loud, shocked chuckle.

"You're Hannah's husband?" he asked, that same shock still very present in those three words.

Grant smiled. "Yes, I'm the luckiest man in the world."

Jake laughed. "Well, shit, friend, we need to take you out for a drink!" Grant thought he heard Jake mutter something like, "And I thought I was in shovel trouble."

"We?" Grant asked.

Jake nodded. "My buddy Cal, who does the cabins. We were going to the Crow's Nest tonight for a beer. Usually we go to Goonies, Hannah's place, but I think a change of scene may be good for you."

Jake seemed like a good guy, and truth be told, Grant could use a drink. As well as intel on his wife from people who seemed to know her.

"Hannah's a great woman. Didn't know any man could tie her down, though," Jake said.

"Is that why you're asking me out for a drink? Out of pity?"

Jake smiled. "Not pity—more like camaraderie. I hope the odds are in your favor. But also, my wife is your wife's best friend. And the minute I tell her that I met you today, she will want to know everything and scold me for not making friends."

"Ah, well, I guess that makes sense."

Jake was still smiling. "You'll catch up on the secret rules of marriage here soon." Jake smacked his back. "And I can't wait to get details on how you managed to court her with your balls still intact!"

Honestly, Grant didn't know, either. His wife was a feisty one. But talking about her like this, like a normal man talking to a friend, made him feel like a part of something for the first time. Like . . . community. Family. Plus, Jake was married to Hannah's best friend? That was kind of perfect. He wanted to be a part of Hannah's life, and these people were important to her. Jake was also a cool guy.

Grant picked out a screen door, and Jake smiled. "Should I deliver this to Hannah's place?"

Grant nodded. "That would be great. And I think I'll need a bouquet of flowers, too."

"Ah, man." Jake laughed. "Hannah landed herself a secret husband who gives her flowers? She's going to be so pissed when everyone finds out."

Grant smiled. Anything that would annoy his wife wasn't exactly a bad thing.

* * *

"Five thousand dollars in a week and a half?" Laura asked, swiveling on her bar stool. After Hannah had told her the gist of her problem, she was counting on her best friend to be creative with ways to earn money, since she was the most capable person Hannah knew and might be able to pull something like this off. And because she was the bestest friend ever, Laura had rushed over from her store to come brainstorm and have a sweet tea in Hannah's bar.

Laura tapped her chin and said, "What about a bake sale?"

"I can't bake."

Laura pursed her lips. "True."

"And I'm not a seventh grader raising money for camp. I'm trying to buy a bar."

"Well, we're just brainstorming here," Laura said in her "don't give up hope" tone. This was why Hannah had people like Laura in her life. Because she hoped enough for both of them. Her thoughts turned to Grant. He was a hoper, too. He was also stubborn and relentless—and ruthless, even. Not to mention sexy and caring and—

"I need more ideas," Hannah said, interrupting her train of thought, because it was heading from PG to R in about two seconds.

"Can you knit? Crochet? Ooh! Repurpose old dressers into TV stands?"

Hannah just stared at her friend. "You really need to stop going on Pinterest. It's a form of online addiction, you know."

"But everything is so cute and crafty!" Laura defended with a wistful smile.

"Do I look like a crafter?"

Laura looked her over long and hard like she had back when they were in second grade, deciding if she wanted to be friends and play on the monkey bars. Only now, Hannah was hoping she could help her with a real bar.

"You may not be a crafter, but you have other talents."

Hannah wasn't so sure. She put her forehead in her hand and twirled her whiskey. She was so close to getting what she'd always wanted. What she'd worked for. Her own business, in her small town, stable and middle class. Where she'd always prayed to be. Not trash. Not scraping by. Not just a bartender. And not Silas Hastings's daughter.

"I just need a win," she said.

Laura nodded. "Is everything going okay with your dad?"

Hannah shot her head up. "How do you know?"

"Small town," Laura said softly.

Great. The gossip train was still in full gear. Not that it was surprising—Hannah just hated talking about her dad. Or how regularly she had to bail him out of jail.

"Everything is fine. I just need . . ."

Grant.

She didn't know why his name smashed into her head. Because he was complicating her life more. She was playing his game for now, only so he'd leave and be gone for good. So why couldn't she stop thinking about last night?

Because it had been good.

Really damn good.

"Have you talked to Grant about it?" Laura said, as if reading her mind.

"There's nothing to talk about. This is my bar I'm trying to get with my money."

"He's your husband."

"Not for long," Hannah mumbled.

Laura frowned. "Really? You won't even entertain the idea of staying with him?"

"To do what? We have different lives in different places. It was impulsive, and he's basically blackmailing me. Romantic, huh?"

"Actually, it kind of sounds like it," Laura said with a grin and took a sip of her tea. "Jake and I play forbidden strangers. Where he walks into a place he knows I'm at and we pretend that we're first meeting and then—"

"Go bone in his truck. Yeah, I'm aware of your game," Hannah said.

"Well, you should try it. Maybe it'll be a nice change out of the grouchy pants you're constantly wearing."

Hannah smiled and took a drink of her whiskey. She loved Laura. Her bright, go-get-'em attitude and all. But the situation with her and Grant was different. Difficult. And not some fairy tale. She couldn't help but wonder, though, what that fairy tale would be like. Laura was her best friend and a good resource. Maybe she should talk about her situation with Grant? Get some insight? She'd never talked shop about marriage before and had no clue what being a wife even meant. She'd married Grant out of haste and longing.

She remembered how that fire had felt in her stomach when she thought of losing him. Never seeing him again. Maybe she'd had heatstroke on that ship, but deep, deep down, she knew that would just be another in the long line of excuses she'd thought of over the past half a year.

"You say I'm grouchy like you've never been grouchy with Jake," Hannah offered, trying to sneakily set up a conversation.

"Oh, I've been full-on pissed with Jake, but that's not what marriage is about."

"Is it about who wins the fight?" Hannah asked, genuinely wanting to know.

Laura laughed. "Of course not. It's about knowing what you're fighting for and knowing when to back down."

Hannah didn't do well with backing down. "Like compromise and all that crap?"

"Compromise is a big part of it, but mostly it's waking up every day and making a choice, while also realizing that he wakes up every day and has a choice. And if you start and end every moment knowing your choice is him, then that's when you fight for each other. Because marriage is hard."

Hannah glanced away. She'd had a lot of choices in her life. Several involving Grant. And Grant had a lot of choices when it came to her. He was here. In her town, home, and bed. He was waking up making those choices, and Hannah was sleeping on them.

"It's scary," Laura said, as if reading her mind. "Because marriage is trusting someone to show up and choose you every day."

Hannah didn't have great experience with that. She'd never had her parents in her corner, or even Laura all of the time. Hannah had been left, forgotten, or flat-out ignored. Yet from the moment she met Grant, he'd made her feel seen.

A loud breath pushed past her lips of its own will. Her mind was in knots and her stomach fizzing because she hadn't remembered to inhale through this conversation. Which meant she needed to change topics.

"I can't even begin to deal with the Grant situation right now. I need to get this bar before I ever have a chance to lose it."

"Maybe you're trying to do everything yourself again. Getting support isn't a bad thing. Counting on someone else isn't a bad thing, either," Laura said.

"Hey, I called you, didn't I?"

"Yes, but you know I'm talking about more. You always handle everything yourself. Sure, you called me, but you're taking this burden all on yourself, one hundred percent. You never let anyone in enough to take some of your struggle."

"That's because I'm fine," Hannah defended. "And my struggles are just that—mine. I just need ideas on how to raise money." She didn't mean to snap at Laura, but she couldn't handle the way this conversation was going. It was her own fault for letting it derail in the first place. Because she knew full well that *Grant* was the key issue here. And Hannah just needed something, for once, to go right.

"It's possible, right?" Hannah asked, doing the mental math of what five thousand dollars in ten days would take. Only five hundred bucks a day . . .

She looked around the bar. A bar that wasn't hers but felt like it was. Felt like she was so close to being stable, set, and happy. Being successful and more than just a bartender. More than her father's daughter.

"Anything is possible," Laura said with all the can-do attitude only a former prom queen could have. Her cell phone buzzed, and Laura flipped a lock of blonde hair over her shoulder and started tapping on it. Likely texting Jake, because she was smiling at the screen like a moron. If she started talking about love and babies and world peace, Hannah was going to take the nearest fork and stick it in her ear hole.

Babies.

Why had that word entered her brain?

First comes love, then comes marriage, then comes baby in the baby carriage.

Hannah wanted to laugh at her own internal absurdity. She had the marriage, wasn't sure about the love, and babies? Hell no. She was way too terrified to be a mother. Too many risk factors for messing up a kid. Funny—she had a husband, and they'd never discussed family.

Not that she would be having that discussion any time soon. Jesus, she needed to stop thinking about Grant. Because the more she thought of him and the situation she found herself in, the more those thoughts expanded into questions . . . particularly about the future.

She needed a break tonight. On the outskirts of town, there was a big dance hall bar.

"I think we just need to get creative. And the best way to do that is to clear the mind of stress and relax," Laura said, putting her cell phone away after what seemed to be a happy texting exchange.

Hannah frowned. "Why do I feel like you're on the brink of trying to talk me into something?"

Laura faked a shocked breath and held a hand to her heart. "I would never . . . ," she said with so much embellishment, Hannah could smell the sweetness coating each word.

"I just think you need a break, and coming out with me tonight is perfect. We can go out, have fun, dance, and just relax and let loose a little. That's when the ideas will hit."

"Uh-huh," Hannah said in a bored tone. "Surely they'll hit due to 'relaxing' and not the five drinks you always end up having whenever we have girls' night and you get a hold of cheap vodka and an open mic."

"Hey, people love my rendition of Shania Twain."

Hannah shook her head and smiled. "Whatever you say."

"So you'll come with me?" she asked.

Hannah could use an excuse to stay out of the house tonight and not deal with Grant. Because every time she thought of him, she thought of him *naked*. Which meant that being around him wasn't the best idea.

"Yeah, I'm in," she said.

Laura clapped lightly and took an adorable sip of her tea. "Good! Then wear your most sexy outfit."

"Sexy outfit?" Hannah said. "I have jeans or jeans."

"No, you have a dress. I saw it in your closet last month."

Hannah immediately knew which dress she was talking about. The tight blue one that she'd worn the night she met Grant on the cruise ship.

"So dig out that dress, put it on, and figure out who you want to be tonight, because we're going out to get creative," Laura said with a smile.

Hannah was hit with an instant dose of déjà vu that she had a feeling would bite her in the ass tonight.

Chapter Five

Hannah was on her second drink, and the dress she wore felt foreign against her skin. The last time she'd worn it, she'd been with the man who was now making her life complicated.

"You look great," Laura said as she picked up her fruity pink drink off the bar and glanced around. She was in a dress as well and looked way more comfortable than Hannah felt. They were at the Crow's Nest. The big bar held dance lessons, events, and concerts. Not massive, but not small like Goonies. It was the main place people came when they wanted to have more than just a drink in a bar. They wanted to move. And although Hannah wasn't a dancer, the upbeat swing of the band playing popular cover songs made her toes tap and her hips sway just a little.

"Don't look now, but I think you're starting to relax," Laura said.

Hannah just raised a brow and looked around at all the people. The place was packed, and she was actually liking being out in the world beyond her home, Goonies, or Main Street.

She hadn't seen Grant when she'd gone home to change earlier. And she was wondering what he was doing. Wondering if he was thinking of her. Not that she cared. And she definitely hadn't spent the better part of her shift today watching the front door wondering if he'd walk through it.

Had he gone back to New York?

She hadn't checked the house for his things. She'd just hustled in and left after a quick change, some eyeliner and lipstick, and a fluff of the hair. But surely he wouldn't leave without saying goodbye . . .

I thought you wanted him gone?

Her mind was a whispering bitch. Hannah downed her drink in one swallow.

"You look so sad all of a sudden," Laura said.

"Nope, I'm good, just need another drink."

"Are you thinking of the money for the bar? We'll find a way. Don't worry."

Surprisingly, Hannah hadn't been thinking of that. She'd been thinking of Grant. Wondering if this pain in her chest would ever stop pulsing.

"Miss?" the bartender called to Hannah. She turned and faced him. He slid her a drink—the exact drink she'd just consumed. "Gentleman over there bought you ladies a round," the bartender said, placing a replica of Laura's drink next to Hannah's on the bar top.

Hannah frowned at the glass as she picked it up. She took a seat on the bar stool. That's when she noticed Laura looking over her shoulder, giving a little wave, and blowing a kiss. Ah, she must see Jake. They were probably playing one of their little "pretend to be strangers" games.

Hannah rolled her eyes and glanced over and saw—

"Fuck me," Hannah breathed.

It was Grant. Standing right behind her.

"Maybe later," he said and winked. "But first I was hoping to buy you a drink and get to know you. Hi, my name is Grant Laythem."

Hannah looked at him like he'd lost his mind. But then she saw Jake walk up next to him and say something like an introduction to Laura.

Ah, crap. Not only were they playing a game, somehow Hannah had gotten roped into it.

"So, what, you're best friends with Jake now?"

Grant frowned at her. "Oh, you know my friend Jake? I had no idea," he said, clearly sarcastic. Judging by how chummy the two men were, she could now guess where Grant had spent his day—at the home goods store.

"Are you seriously trying to be best friends with my best friend's husband?" she asked in disbelief.

"I'm doing no such thing," Grant said in a sweet, defensive tone. Great, now he was mocking her. "Turns out, I'm approachable."

Before Hannah could roll her eyes again, Jake slung an arm around Grant's broad shoulders. "This guy here is my brother from another mother," he said. Laura giggled; Hannah gagged. This game was already going too far. But it looked like Jake was serious. Grant and he had really become friends? Not only was Grant inserting himself into her life—in more ways than one—now he was wandering around town and making friends with her friends. Moreover, those friends seemed to like him a lot. Which made sense, since Grant was a force. Good luck running into him and not being enchanted. Hannah was still trying to shake the effects he had on her. A feat not going so well, considering she was still married to the bastard and he was in her town, her house, and her bed.

All signs of permanence. Which made her chest tighten, and she couldn't figure out if it was in terror or desperation. The hope that maybe he was serious about making their relationship work. Maybe he really could stick around and they could be together—

Stop.

She needed to stop this thinking. Clearly it was the alcohol swirling in her brain and not her real thoughts.

"She's surprised I'm so likable," Grant said to Jake, as if she couldn't hear him.

"Maybe if you weren't such a pain in the ass all the time, I'd believe your likability a bit more," she countered and took a swig of her drink. Grant's eyes were on her the entire time. Heat burned down her neck from his intense stare, even deeper than the burn of the alcohol flowing down her throat.

"You haven't gotten a chance to really know my ass, or the pain I can bring yours," he said with a wink. But his voice was rough and deep, and the seriousness in it made her skin prickle with anticipation.

Maybe this game wouldn't be so bad . . .

"I wanted to come introduce myself," he continued, "because you are the most beautifully stubborn woman I've ever seen."

"How in the hell would you know any of that?" she challenged, meeting his "getting to know you" ruse head-on.

"Because I just saw that beautiful face twist with pain, then you mentally told yourself to fuck off."

Hannah's mouth dropped open. Either Grant was a psychic, or he read her better than she'd ever guessed.

"I . . . I was just thinking. There's no way you could know what about."

He grinned. Holding his tumbler of liquor between two fingers, he casually leaned against the bar, making him the focal point of Hannah's entire position. And goddamn it, the man looked good. Dark blue jeans, black belt, and white button-down rolled at the sleeves. Still classy casual. Just like Grant.

"I think you were thinking of me. Missing me, even," he said quietly next to her ear.

"How would you know that? We're strangers, I thought?" she said, glancing at Jake and Laura, who were clearly playing out their own roles only a few feet away.

"Ah, so nice to meet you then, stranger."

Shit. By saying that, Grant had trapped Hannah in role-playing, and she'd now basically offered to play along. Fantastic . . .

They were in the middle of this couples' game, and Hannah wanted to tell both of the lovebirds where they could go.

Instead, she looked Grant over. He wanted to play? Fine. She could play.

And she'd win.

∽

"Well, it's nice to meet you, Gary. I'm Hannah," his wife said to him, and then she shook his hand. Nice touch getting his name wrong on purpose. Brat. Sexy brat, but a brat nonetheless.

Despite his wife being her usual difficult self, Grant felt a swell of pride that the advice Jake had given him earlier might actually pay off. Hannah was on board with this little game, and Grant was excited to take full advantage. He'd have to thank Jake later for the great idea.

"May I sit?" he asked.

She kicked the open stool out for him. Laura was laughing and saying something into Jake's ear. Those two started to flirt and headed toward the dance floor. Leaving a blessed moment of privacy between Grant and the woman he'd come to see.

"So, Glenn, tell me why a guy like you is in a town like this," Hannah asked, facing him and taking a confident swallow of her drink. The woman was sexy and sinful, and if she wanted to get under his skin by getting his name wrong, she had another think coming. Because he'd make her yell his name tonight when she begged him for more.

"It's Grant," he said. "And I'm here trying to find something I've been missing."

Hannah nodded. "Sounds mysterious."

He shrugged. "More difficult than mysterious."

She glared. Yep, he'd just called her difficult to her face. He was ready for her to break character any moment, but she didn't.

"Well, you must be excited to get back home to the city," she said.

"How do you know I'm from the city?" He took a drink and enjoyed watching her pretty eyes run the length of him. Just her hot gaze was enough to get him hard.

"It's obvious," she finally said.

"A lot of things about you are obvious as well," he countered.

Her throat bobbed, and her strong stare wavered. She looked like she'd lost a touch of confidence when she uttered, "Like?"

He never wanted her feeling anything but confident. Just like the night he'd met her—he'd seen right away how strong she was. Yet with that kind of steady strength came a loneliness behind her eyes, and he hated seeing that. Would do anything to chase it away. So he told her what he'd thought of her the moment he met her, which still rang true tonight.

He placed a single hand on her knee briefly, then took it away. "You're beautiful. Straight to your soul kind of beauty. So powerful I can see it alive in your eyes."

Her lips parted briefly, and Grant loved that she seemed to like his honesty. Because he was honest, damn it. Hannah was a uniquely beautiful person. Which was why he'd fallen in love with her so quickly.

"I'm also told I'm a pain in the ass," she said.

Oh, she absolutely was, but that's why he loved her. That's why she was special in a way that he'd never found in another woman. Hannah was a fighter, even when she was a lover. Never just one—always everything.

"I have no doubt," Grant agreed.

She laughed into her glass before taking another swallow. What he'd give to taste the whiskey on her lips in that moment. And her in that dress made him think of the night in the Blue Bar. She'd been wearing the same dress. Blue. Showing off all her curves and accenting her eyes. A waterfall of black hair and painted lips made him want to taste her.

With her looking at him like that and the soft scent of ocean air, he could almost convince himself that were back on that ship.

"Well, I hope you find what you're missing and that it actually is something you can take with you."

He looked at her for a long moment. They both knew he was talking about Hannah. Knew she was what he'd been looking for. What he wanted.

"That's my plan," he told her.

She brushed off his words with a soft cough and changed the subject. "You have family in New York?" she asked.

"Yes. My mother." This wasn't what he wanted to talk about. He wanted to play with Hannah and talk about her. Get her to cave and admit she still had feelings—strong feelings—for him.

"And your dad?" she pressed. That single question made Grant's ribs twitch. He wasn't prepared to talk about his dad. So he stuck to blunt, quick facts.

"He died a few months ago."

Her eyes shot wide and fastened on him. "I'm so sorry."

There was a genuine concern in her voice, and Grant wondered if they weren't playing anymore. Because she looked truly sad for him. How did she do that? One look at those expressive eyes made his chest raw, like his heart was beating on the outside of his body. Fleshy and vulnerable and on display. His mouth watered with the need to speak, but he didn't. While he should open up—he felt the overwhelming thump in his throat to talk more—he held back. Not tonight. Because the way she looked at him had him thinking he'd tell her everything.

Instead, he'd be patient and stick to simplistic responses for now.

"Thank you. He was a good man." Grant tried to get off this topic. It was his turn to take a drink, because this pretend game felt very real.

Hannah leaned in and put her hand on his hand. "Will you tell me about him?"

Grant looked at her. He hadn't spoken about his father to anyone since he passed. No good friends he could share experience with. He definitely couldn't talk to his mom. And he found himself wanting to share this piece of himself with Hannah. With his wife. Because it was Hannah who kept giving him *that* look. Like she genuinely cared. Maybe a few details wouldn't be so bad. He could keep himself in check.

"Even though he got screwed over by a woman, he was a romantic at heart," he began. Hannah's lovely eyes fixed to his face. "He took calculated risks—never anything too brazen, though. He always made time for me."

"You are his only son?"

Grant nodded. "Yes. And I've never lost anyone before. The weight of feeling like he's in me, and I carry him where I go is . . ."

"Daunting," Hannah finished. Like she understood.

"Yes."

He looked at her for a long moment, and if he didn't know any better, he'd think he saw pain streak across her face. But it was gone as soon as it came.

"He'll always be a part of you. You're lucky you have a good memory to recall," she said.

Grant nodded. "I am lucky in many ways." He gripped her hands. "Is your dad still alive?"

"Yep," Hannah said quickly, then went back to her drink, slipping her hand away from his. Clearly she didn't want to talk about it, but that made Grant want to know even more. Was this how she felt about him? Pressing him for details about his life because she was interested, just like he was interested in hers? He fucking hoped so. Because he wanted to know her. And continue to know her for the rest of his life. Starting with right now. Just one moment when she'd open up to him. Even if it was the smallest, silliest detail.

"What's your favorite memory with him?" he asked her.

She shook her head. "I don't know. None."

"There has to be one."

She blew out an obviously annoyed breath. Grant could read the moment a memory flashed to mind, because it played over her entire face.

"SpaghettiOs," she said. "I was eight, and he bought me those name-brand SpaghettiOs one time when I was sick. I had a stomach bug in third grade. But I ate them and I remember smiling even when my stomach hurt so bad, because it was the only time I got to eat those. And he bought them for me."

Grant nodded. There was so much Hannah kept close to her chest. So much she cut off. But tonight, he saw a glimpse of the woman he'd met on the cruise ship. The one who had opened up to him. And he wanted to see more.

"Is that why you have a cupboard full of it?" he asked. Her eyebrows shot up in question, and Grant shrugged. "I've been staying with you, remember? I was looking for food and saw four cans in there."

She gave a short laugh. "I never really thought about it. I only eat them when I'm sick. Weird, I know. Tomato sauce and pasta made for kids, and it's the only thing I want."

"Because it comforts you. That's not weird at all."

Hannah frowned. "My father has never comforted me, so don't go getting analytical on me, Freud."

"I'm not trying to. I just like knowing the different ways to your heart. Now that I have the inside scoop, forget diamonds and flowers—I'm getting you canned soup and whiskey."

She laughed, her eyes crinkling at the sides from pure joy. "You know me so well."

That hit Grant in the gut. He did know her, and she'd just admitted it. But it wasn't because of his joke—it was because he knew how to make her laugh, and when. Pride filled his muscles like a dose of steroids, and he was stronger from having made his wife happy tonight. It was the best victory he could have hoped for.

Hope.

That theme was ticking through every second of every day Grant was on the clock, trying to win his wife back.

He wanted to ask her more, to make her laugh again, to have her admit that he was the right man for her, but before he could ask for just that, she cut him off.

"So what do you do, Glenn?"

They were still in game mode, so he'd continue to play. He smiled, loving her sass even now, and with the squaring of her shoulders, he could tell she was back to playing her part, trying to go for surface questions. But Grant could dig deeper using only a surface tool.

"I'm in business."

"No shit," she said in a bored tone. "That could mean anything from you work at a dry cleaner's to you're in the mob."

"Somewhere in the middle. But closer to dry cleaner."

She laughed. And he missed that sound. Her happy. He tried to remember how many times he'd made her laugh on the cruise ship. A lot. But she didn't seem the same. Either the past six months had been tough on her, or his wife's life here in this small town maybe wasn't what she wanted. He could only hope to push her to move to New York with him.

One step at a time...

He had to get her to admit she liked him first.

Then admit she still loved him.

"What do you do?" he asked, changing the topic on her.

"I own a bar," she said confidently.

"That right?"

She glanced away. "Well, I will soon. Just a few details I'm ironing out." She glared at him. "And I'm also dealing with some legal matters so no one can claim what's mine."

So she was still pissed about his little blackmail stunt. He would never take her bar or her dreams. He wanted to help. He used what he had to in order to get a second chance with her. But once again, there was a lot he couldn't say out loud. For now, she could be pissy with him about this, because it got him the two weeks he wanted. Well, one week and, come tomorrow, five days. Time was already dwindling fast.

"The bar down on Main Street?" he asked, sticking to character. "That's a cool place. Looks busy. Would be a good investment opportunity."

"Yeah, if only I could get the whole investment," she mumbled. Grant was pretty sure he wasn't meant to hear that, but he did. Hannah needed money? Help? He wanted to spring into action and save the day, but if there was one thing he knew about his wife, it was that her pride was important.

"Oh my gosh, I've got it!" Laura said loudly, inserting herself between Grant and Hannah, clearly having had at least two drinks in the past fifteen minutes. Judging by the sway in her step, she must be feeling tipsy. "What if we throw a parade?"

Hannah frowned, and so did Grant.

"It's okay, Laura, we'll talk about this later," Hannah said quietly.

"No, no, I mean it. There's a ton of money to be made in parades!"

Yep, Hannah's friend was drunk and also confirming what Grant had thought: Hannah needed money to buy her bar.

"Let's talk about this tomorrow," Hannah said, and Laura danced to the music and sipped her pink drink and went back to Jake near the dance floor.

Grant didn't want to ask for details—he wanted to help. And Hannah would never let him. But he had to be sure what the hell she was talking about. He knew money talk, and that was obviously the prime issue here. He still needed more details on just what Hannah was struggling with and what she was hiding. He had to be sly about uncovering this, though, because he was very aware of his wife's pride.

"So you're in the parade business now?"

Hannah shook her head and ordered two shots of whiskey. Grant was surprised when she slid one his way.

"Don't worry about it. She's just drunk."

Grant nodded. Hannah was definitely keeping her money situation from him. Just like he was from her. Ironic thing was, he could help if she would only let him.

Which meant he'd have to come through with the truth about his financial situation, too. So it looked like he'd have to activate stealth mode and make things happen under the table.

"To new beginnings," he said and held up his shot.

Hannah clanked it. And in one swallow, they both took it.

The band started to play the song "Red Red Wine," and he caught a glimpse of Hannah's smile.

"That was a good night," he said, hoping she was hearing the same lyrics he was and recalling the same thing. She looked at him, and her eyes told him she knew exactly what he was talking about.

"Yeah, it was." She grinned. His wife was a little tipsy, and he liked her playful side coming out. "The cruise had the 'neon drinks and nineties' night."

"Endless booze and all the hits," Grant laughed. They'd played this song on the fifth night he was with Hannah. He remembered it perfectly, and just hearing it now, being face-to-face with her, made his chest tighten.

"Remember those strung-up twinkly lights that started to turn red on the deck when this song game on?" Hannah asked with joy in her tone.

His whole chest tensed, and his blood heated. "I remember."

She'd looked so beautiful in her white dress, dark hair down and flowing. The glow of the flickering light on her skin made him want to taste her all over.

He stood up and held out his hand.

She frowned at it. "What are you doing?"

"I'm taking a stroll down memory lane, and I want my wife to come with me," he said honestly.

She looked at him for a long moment, and Grant was getting worried she'd tell him to fuck off, but she finally took his hand and he led them to the dance floor. He pulled her close and wrapped his arms around her. Feeling her hips sway just like they had six months ago on the ship to this same song.

He breathed in her hair, closed his eyes for a moment, and felt what he knew to be the same love he'd had that night months ago. Hannah was it for him. Fit him perfectly. And he held tighter. Hoping the rest of life and all the complications would somehow work out.

She moved with him. Melted into him. Her skin hot, her sweet voice quietly singing along to the song as she danced with him.

~

Haiti was hot but overcast, and Hannah was walking through her first country outside the United States. The ship had docked a few hours ago, and she'd run off. Well, she'd stealthily walked and was now somewhere between a forest and a beach and . . . She glanced down at her phone. No service. No GPS. No problem—she'd figure it out. The ocean was where the ship was, and surely she could find her way back. She needed the air. She wasn't avoiding Grant. Okay, she kind of was. Only because he was so intense. Rather, he made her feel intensely.

"That doesn't even make sense," she said to herself. More to her inner thoughts. This man made her feel *intensely*? What the hell did that even mean?

She couldn't pinpoint a single emotion, because her whole body was still humming from last night. Feeling his skin, tasting his tongue, hearing his voice right against her ear when he commanded her to come. He was raw and rough and consuming, and she'd loved every minute. Replayed their time together over and over.

Which was stupid.

Because this was only day two on a cruise, and no one could make a connection this fast. She'd come on this trip to get a grip and take control of her life. Because she could only count on herself. She knew better than to fall. In any way. She couldn't fall for her father's endless excuses and con jobs. Couldn't fall for the promises of her boss that one day she could buy the bar she loved. Couldn't fall for Grant just because they'd had a great night. Falling was stupid, because smashing into the ground hurt. And Hannah knew firsthand there would never be anyone to catch her.

She blew a lock of hair out of her face and looked around again. Her skin was sticky from the humidity, and the sky was getting grayer. The ship required all people to be back on board by 5:00 p.m. She had an hour . . . but she couldn't see past the trees.

"How in the hell did I get this lost?" she breathed to herself. She'd wanted a hike, an adventure, and now she was alone. On an island. Figured. Irony never seemed to miss her.

Alone.

And not a soul on earth would know she was missing. Would the boat leave without her? Her breaths came faster, and she started to hustle. In which direction, she didn't know. She just wound through the forest that had looked beautiful an hour ago and now was a prison. The branches scraping her arms, her steps echoing as if reminding her how alone she was.

Her eyes stung, and it had nothing to do with the sea air.

She looked at her phone again. Time was passing, and she had no communication. Not that anyone could help her. What if she didn't make it home? Would her father notice? Maybe, once he sobered up in jail and no one was there to bail him out.

Hannah had never counted on a soul in her life, but she'd give anything to know how it felt to be bailed out. To have someone come through for her.

She hustled faster. She'd be fine. She forced her brain to kick into strength and willpower. *Everything is fine.* She was capable, and she didn't need anyone. She didn't need help. She'd be okay . . .

That sting flared up behind her eyes again, and when she blinked, a single bead of moisture escaped.

Her heart raced, but her blood was sluggish, trying to keep up with the beating in her temples. What was this feeling?

Fear.

I'm scared . . . and alone . . .

She wiped the back of her hand over her eyes and moved faster.

"I'll be okay . . . I'll be okay . . ." But the more she tried to assure herself, the more she felt the opposite. She did the only thing she could—she started humming to herself.

She glanced up and was hit on the forehead with a raindrop. This was bad. Really bad. She shook her head and pressed on. Hoping to God she was going the right way and just praying to break the tree line, where she could hopefully see farther out.

A loud, deep voice sounded in the distance. "Hannah! Are you out there, Hannah?"

Hannah's eyes shot wide. She ran to the voice. "I'm here! Please, don't leave me." She didn't know who was listening, but she begged the voice to help her. To find her.

The trees rustled, and she ran faster toward it. Toward another person. Hoping she was close to the beach—

She ran into a hard chest, and arms instantly surrounded her. Warmth and spice engulfed her. She looked up and saw Grant's eyes burning down on her.

"Are you all right?" he said with an edge in his voice. "I've looked everywhere for you."

"You . . . you have?" She met his eyes and gripped his biceps.

"Of course. I was getting worried."

"But the ship . . . we have to be back in twenty minutes."

"So we'll run. I wasn't leaving without knowing you were safe." His voice was steady, his arms refusing to loosen. He held her. There in the middle of an island.

She wasn't alone.

When Grant leaned in and placed his lips on hers, she realized that for the first time, someone had come for her.

∼

Hannah was falling. Falling in a way she recognized. Because she'd felt the same way when she'd met Grant and in the entire two weeks that followed.

He held her close as they swayed to the music, surrounded by people in a bar pretending to be strangers. But nothing felt strange about being with Grant. It felt right.

His big hands on her drew her closer. One at the small of her back, the other splayed wide in between her shoulder blades. She hugged him back, letting the music move them. Getting lost in him.

His spicy smell and crisp white shirt against her cheek felt familiar.

She wasn't just falling—she was ready to jump.

Off the cliff of reason and right into everything she felt for Grant.

"I'm getting swept up," she said against his chest.

He hugged her closer just as the song ended. "That's not a bad thing," he said.

She looked up at him and was hit with those dark eyes staring back at her. "Isn't it?"

He shook his head. "Not when it feels like this."

He gently lowered his lips to hers, and the kiss was so soft, so perfect, she felt like she could stay right there against this mouth, his body, forever.

"Take me," she breathed against his mouth.

"Take you home?" he asked.

She smiled and bit his lower lip, "Take me anywhere. Just take *me* now."

Understanding clearly hit Grant, and he didn't hesitate. Just grabbed her hand and led her straight out of the bar and toward the parking lot. Hannah had her car. She wasn't worried about Laura. That girl could obviously get a ride home with her husband. Seemed like the boys showed up together, the girls showed up together, and at the end of the night, they paired off.

The crisp sea air cooled her warm cheeks, and she tugged him along the walkway behind the bar toward the ocean.

Once they were several yards away from the bar and down the path, she pinned him against the smooth wood railing and kissed him hard.

She wasn't in charge for long. Grant grabbed her ass and hoisted her up. She instantly wrapped her legs around his waist. He set her down on the top rail, his hard cock still pressing between her thighs. This railing seemed to have been made for them because he hit her perfectly.

"Do you have any idea how much I want you?" he said, rucking her dress up to her waist. The air hit her bare thighs, and her high heels scratched the bottom rung of the railing.

"You keep saying that, but I haven't seen the Grant I remember come out to play yet . . ." She nipped his throat, then kissed him hard.

He drew back just enough to look her in the eyes. The raw ferocity behind those dark pools made her wet and excited.

"You are forgetting last night," he said with a low warning in his tone.

"Last night was nice," she said with an exaggerated shrug. "But I'm talking about how you like it rough."

With him wedged between her thighs, his deep breath made his strong chest graze up, then down, her breasts.

"I thought that was you screaming into the couch," he challenged.

She smiled and kissed his chin. "Yeah, that was me, but I was disappointed. I thought you'd smack my ass and really take me hard.

Like you did on the ship. Over, and over, and over . . ." She trailed her tongue around the seam of his lips. She could feel the hum of his ferocity and knew she was playing a dangerous game. Dangerously sexy. Because Grant loved his control. Loved his dominance. But he was calm and treated her well at the same time. His aggressive side came out when tapped in the right spot, and Hannah was desperate to see that side of him.

"Careful when you use the word *disappoint* with me, Hannah." His tone was low and serious. "Because I'd never disappoint you on purpose."

She knew that. "I loved everything about last night, but I miss the way you used to take me without holding back."

"What makes you think I was holding back?"

She shifted her hips, and he hissed when she rocked against his hard shaft. "Because your hands on me were softer. I miss you clutching me here . . ." She took his hand and had him cup her throat. "And I miss you smacking me here . . ." She took his other hand and lifted herself up just enough to place his palm on her ass. "I mean it when I ask you to take me. Hard. Completely."

"Okay," he said. "First tell me why."

Damn. She was hoping she'd get away with not having to admit that. But clearly Grant wanted to hear it . . . even though he obviously already knew.

"Because I like it," she said softly.

He raised a brow. "Tell me the *entire* reason."

"You're the only one I want . . . the only one I enjoy."

A sexy, sinister grin split his face.

"The only one," he repeated. Not a question. An affirmation.

She nodded. "Yes."

He crashed his mouth down on hers, and Hannah instantly clutched his shoulders. She felt all his hot, wild need engulf her like a fog. This was her man. All of him. The only one who ever made her feel alive. The only one she'd ever let take her over.

Because sometimes it felt good to be dominated. Taken care of. Left in the capable hands of another. Grant did all those things for her. That's why she'd fallen for him the way she did. She trusted he could take all of her and not break her in the process. He was the only one she'd ever been able to give up control to. Not because she was a control freak, but because she'd never trusted another person to come through for her before.

From day one, Grant had made her feel like she was worth chasing.

His hand stayed cupped on her throat, and his thumb pressed against her bottom lip. She bent enough to suck it, and he groaned. The grip on her ass tightened, and when she released his thumb from her lips with a pop, he tugged her low-cut dress down in one hard yank, freeing her breasts instantly.

The cool night air hit her skin, and goose bumps pricked so intensely she could feel each individual chill get heated by Grant's nearness.

With one strong arm wrapped around her waist, he pulled her closer and fused his mouth to her nipple.

"Oh God, yes," she said. She ran her fingers through his hair and held him tight. He sucked hard, his whole face pressed against her breast. She felt his five o'clock shadow scrape against her cleavage as his jaw moved over her skin.

"You want it rough, baby?" he said against her, gently biting her nipple until she hissed and threw her hips out to grind against him.

"Yes!"

"You want all I can give you?" he asked, paying attention to the other nipple. She dug her nails into his scalp and threw her head back. Loving the sting of his bite and the soothing, warm swipe of his tongue to follow.

"Then tell me what I want to hear," he growled. In one swift move, he was back to cupping her throat while his other hand gripped the back of her hair. He yanked, direct but soft. Not hurting her, but enough to show her she was under his control. And she loved it.

Her mouth was open and a millimeter from his. She could taste him. So close, but not close enough.

"What do you want to hear?" she challenged. "What . . . that I missed you?" she scoffed.

He growled, his grip tightening on her hair.

She smiled.

She was goading him on purpose. Loving that every remark brought out more of his power. And she needed to be taken over.

"Oh, you don't like that? You know, I didn't cry once," she said. "I didn't sit around in a depression longing for you."

His eyes narrowed. "Of course you didn't. That's not your style, baby." With his hand still on her throat, he slowly skimmed his thumb along her jaw. "You might not have cried and swooned, but I bet you cursed and raged."

She gasped. All the endless nights over the past six months hitting her at once. The day after she left him, she cussed every time she looked in the mirror. She kicked the door open every day when she came home from work. She threw her sheets off her bed because she couldn't stand them against her skin. They were cold. Too cold.

He was right.

She was in a rage.

Sad rage.

His mouth against her, he whispered, "Tell me how you dealt with it."

She swallowed hard, thinking about just that . . .

How had she dealt with the separation? With missing him. With the rage of needing him.

"You told me last night," he pushed. "Told me you touched yourself thinking of me. Told you haven't been with anyone but me. Because they just aren't good enough for you, are they, baby?"

He slid his hand from her throat to her mouth, trailing his fingers over her lips.

"You thought of me like this . . ." He gave her hair a playful yet curt pull.

She moaned.

"You thought of me taking over . . . owning you . . ." He dipped his first two fingers inside her mouth, and she sucked them. "You know how I know that?"

She shook her head.

He withdrew his fingers from her lips and then put them between her legs, right at her opening. "Because I remember you begging me for it. Loving how you submitted to me. And I gave you what you wanted, didn't I?"

"Yes," she whispered. His fingers teasing her opening. She shifted her hips, trying to get him to put them inside.

"Greedy girl," he said. "Before you get what you want, tell me what I want to hear."

She met his eyes. "I did want it. I still do. You're the only one . . ."

"The only one what?" he said through clenched teeth. She knew what he wanted to hear. Knew they'd been dancing around this, and she had to admit it. Would implode from need or heat if she couldn't have him.

"You're the only one I've ever loved."

The moment the last word slipped out of her mouth, Grant slid those two wet fingers inside her all the way to the hilt.

"Oh God, Grant," she muttered; her head fell forward, and she bit down on his shoulder.

His entire body shifted, or maybe it was his mood. Or both. Because while he still held that power she loved so much, there was that deep care in him that she trusted. Grant wouldn't hurt her. Wouldn't let her fall. Wouldn't deny her. She knew that. Bone-deep, she truly believed that.

With his free hand, he grabbed her wrist and placed her hand on the top of his head, tangling her fingers into his hair.

"Do not let go," he said.

She nodded and held tight to his hair as he slid down to his knees. With his fingers still deep inside her, he opened her legs wider and buried his face between her thighs.

She gasped and gripped his hair tighter. She used her free hand to grip the rail she sat on to steady herself. Fire lit up her body as Grant's skilled tongue snaked over her center.

She clamped her legs against his face, then spread them wider, then clamped. She needed more. But it was too much. The pleasure was like flecks of hot light pricking her, and she was coming out of her skin with lust.

"Grant, oh please, please . . ." She was begging him. Just like he said she had. Just like she was currently doing. But he kept her right on the edge. Literally.

He thrust his fingers in and out, faster and deeper each time. Her core slickened. His tongue flicked fast over the sensitive bundle of nerves, and she arched and moved, gripping him so tight when she thought she'd fall.

But she didn't.

Grant was right there.

A strong arm around her, steadying her while he drove her to a lust-crazed frenzy.

"Come for me, baby," he growled between her legs. He plunged deep, and she did.

Her body convulsed and tensed around the most powerful orgasm she'd had since . . .

Since she'd last been with Grant.

She called his name. Screamed it? She didn't know. She was lost to the fire raging through her veins and the pleasure humming deep in her bones.

He rose to stand, and Hannah felt limp. Her skin buzzing, and her mind in a whirl of fog and lust.

And once again, Grant was there to catch her. Hold her. Not let her fall.

"You're not worn out yet, are you, baby?" he said against her lips.

She said no, or maybe she thought it. Her brain was nothing more than bursting fireworks, and her skin was crackling with wanting his hands all over it. Truth was, her body was needy and spent at the same time. The aftershocks of pleasure were still spiraling while she desperately wanted Grant inside her.

"Please," she whispered.

His face was against hers, his lips brushing hers. He gripped the back of her head in one hand, tangling her hair through his fingers, and tugged. Her chin lifted, and through her lashes, she saw his eyes burning into her soul.

"Please what?" he asked.

Please take me, own me, love me.

She had so many requests. She wanted to feel that calm safety that Grant gave her. Complete. There, by the ocean and surrounded by the entire world and her small town all at once, she didn't feel alone. She needed to feel him for a little longer.

"Finish me," she said.

His grip tightened, and he kissed her deep. His tongue was hot and sweet in her mouth, drinking her down with each stroke. His strong jaw worked against her cheek, his shaven face like fine sandpaper against her.

She knew every part of him, and she knew how all of those parts felt against her. Her eyes were squeezed shut, and her fingers were digging into his shoulders, yet she could still see the entire scene as if she floated above her body. Picturing his strong back and broad shoulders moving and bunching with muscles as he snaked his free arm around her waist and pulled her into him. Her legs spread wider, his hips digging into her inner thighs. His hard cock was hot and urgent against her slick flesh. She wanted his pants gone so she could feel him skin to skin.

Her hands roamed from his back to his sides, then up his chest. In one fierce tug, she opened his shirt, buttons flying, and Grant growled against her lips.

"Finish you, huh?" he said, then sucked her tongue quickly. "What if I'm never finished with you?"

He kissed down her neck, sucking and biting as he went. Her heels slipped against the railing, so she wrapped her legs around his waist. She reached between them and opened his belt, then his pants.

She reached into his jeans and grabbed his cock, pulling it free. She used her feet to shove his pants low, giving her better access. She was frantic, like a live wire popping in a rainstorm. She needed to touch him everywhere. Feel him everywhere.

"I miss this," he growled against her throat. He yanked her closer while thrusting. She felt his cock slide in her hand and hit her clit. He was right there but didn't push to be inside her.

"You can have it, just come here," she whispered and wiggled her hips while trying to guide him into her. But he shifted, only sliding along her wet center.

"Oh, I will, and I do miss your sweet pussy, but I meant that I miss *this*..." He clung to her tighter. She kissed his neck, his cheek, his lips. "I miss you loving on me."

His words hung between them, dancing from his breath to hers. She'd missed this, too. The need and ache and soft fall into him. She didn't know what to say. Worried that whatever she tried to say would be exactly wrong, or perfectly right. So she kissed him. Closed her lips over his. She released his cock and wrapped her arms around him, hugging him close. That was all he needed, because she felt that hot steel surge deep inside her.

"Home," he whispered against her ear. So low and soft she almost missed it. Was he telling her he missed his home? Telling her she was his home? She hoped for the latter but didn't want to get swept up.

He stayed buried deep and stirred. Clutching her close, keeping her immobile against him. He had her pinned between the ledge and himself, and he owned her. Took her exactly as he wanted, just like she wanted. Deep, hard, and consuming.

He was hitting the spot inside that made stars dance behind her eyes, and she kissed him.

"This what you wanted, baby?" he asked.

She nodded, tracing his lips with her tongue. Her blood simmered, her bones rattled with the orgasm that was creeping up on her.

He thrust deeper but never pulled away. He was taking her from the inside out, and she had no idea where her skin stopped and his body continued. Complete.

Home...

She felt that word settle into her stomach like it belonged there. Like Grant was the new definition of that single syllable. She couldn't reason with her own thoughts, because her skin started pricking and her toes tingled. Pleasure surged from the middle of her spine through every vein until she burned up.

"I'm coming," she breathed. Then Grant's name was on her lips. A chant, a prayer, she didn't know, but he was the only thing she understood.

"I feel you, baby. I'm with you." He buried his face in her hair and hugged her like he'd never see her again. His body tensed, and with his cock deep inside her, she caught every ounce of pleasure that shot through him.

She didn't know what she mumbled next. She just knew she was spent.

Grant had succeeded in making her beg and barter, and now he'd exhausted her into a sex-induced coma.

Chapter Six

She still loves me . . .

Grant hadn't gotten that thought out of his head since Hannah had uttered those words to him a few nights ago.

And what a night that had been.

He wanted Hannah more than damn near anything, and the way she pushed him, wanted to see all of him, made him want to give it. And he wanted to give her more. But she'd been tired, and in her defense, he had exhausted her.

He smiled and gave himself a mental high five that he still got his wife off so well that she almost lapsed into unconsciousness from the pleasure.

That's when she'd said it . . .

"I love you."

He replayed those words over and over and over.

It had been present tense and the most honest, best thing he'd ever heard in his life. He missed hearing it from her. Missed knowing it. But he did know it. Deep down, she loved him, and that was the hope he kept clinging to. And his stubborn wife was giving him crumbs to add to that hope.

"You talented son of a bitch," Jake said from the other side of the pool table.

Grant stood, holding his pool stick after nailing a perfect shot. "This is a pretty great way to spend a lunch hour," Grant said to his friend.

"Not so great for Jake, since he's losing," Gabe said from the corner, looking over the balls spread out on the table. Grant had met the deputy through Jake and Cal at the Crow's Nest a few nights back. Since then, the guys had invited him out for their weekly Wednesday lunch session, which was a beer, a game, and catching up midweek to make plans for the weekend. Grant was liking this idea of . . . friends. He was seeing why people enjoyed genuine relationships with others. It was why he'd fallen for Hannah so far and fast. Now seeing her town and the people she'd grown up with, he was getting the notion that spending time in a place you loved with people who cared could have advantages over a big, cold city with a heartless mother and endless business discussions.

"Cal is still showing up, right?" Grant asked as Jake leaned in to take his shot.

"Yeah, I think he's preparing his portfolio, though," Gabe said. The man was nice and apparently well known around town. Jake kept calling him MEB, which stood for Most Eligible Bachelor.

"That guy has talent. I saw that subdivision he's working on when I drove around the other day," Grant said and took a drink from his longneck. He had chatted with Cal about an investment opportunity and told him he'd be happy to discuss his business. But this business didn't feel like the cold New York he normally dealt with. He knew these men—at least, he was getting to know them—and he cared.

Jake shanked a shot, and Gabe laughed. "Your game is going to hell."

"Says the guy who struck out with my wife last year," Jake razzed.

Gabe just shook his head. "And I still can't sleep at night," he teased back.

Grant frowned. "Wait . . . are you being serious?"

Both men looked at him then laughed. "Yeah, kind of," Gabe said. "When Laura came back to town a while back, I made a run at her. We had our high school history, after all. Not like the band dork over here." He hiked a thumb at Jake.

"Band dork who can play a clarinet while kicking your ass."

It was clear the guys were still joking, but Grant really wanted to ask more questions. They'd all gone to school together and, at some point, had overcome differences. He wondered what having friends and a sense of belonging felt like.

"This is just incredible," Grant said, leaning against the pool table.

"What's that?" Jake asked, his massive arms bulging from his T-shirt when he placed his palms on the edge of the pool table.

"How you all know each other."

Gabe laughed. "You make it sound like you grew up on Mars."

"No, just very different. I can see why Hannah connects the way she does."

Both men frowned and exchanged a glance. "Connects?" Gabe asked.

"Yeah, the first day I met her, she just had this kind of open personality that drew me in." Gabe glanced down, and it concerned Grant. "You know Hannah in a different way?"

"Hannah has had a rough life," Gabe said. "She's tough, but she has a big vulnerability."

Jake nodded.

"What do you mean? Her bar?"

Gabe shook his head. "Her dad. She has more patience and love than anyone I've ever known. But she'll rip your balls off, too."

Grant knew that to be true, but hearing this from people who'd known her since she was young made his heart rise in his chest. He wanted to know her like that. He was grateful he knew her in other ways. But Hannah kept what hurt her close, and Grant understood that. He just wanted to tap into that piece of her and learn her more.

Before he could get more info, Cal walked in.

"Hey, guys!" he called, weaving around the pool tables. He headed straight to Grant and shook his hand.

"Thanks so much for meeting me," Cal said.

The soft sound of wind chimes sang from the door being opened and closed. A fresh dose of sea air wafted around. Grant could smell the saltwater taffy from the candy shop down the street on the breeze.

"Glad we could meet again," he said. Cal placed his portfolio on the table next to Grant's beer.

"Do you guys need another round?" Cal asked.

"I'm good, thanks," Jake said.

"Me, too. How's the building going?" Gabe said.

Cal smiled and tapped his portfolio. "Good. Grant and I have been chatting."

"We've heard," Jake said with a wink. "You're giddier than you were on prom night before picking up Debbie Alberts."

"Well, I am a handsome man," Grant joked.

They all laughed.

"I'm going to get a drink," Cal said. "Feel free to dig into that." He pointed at the portfolio. With a smile, he headed to the counter and ordered.

Grant opened the file and started looking through it. Cal's business was all laid out; the entire business plan was solid . . .

"He's really talented," Gabe said, glancing at the portfolio.

Grant nodded in agreement. "Yeah, he is."

"I work with the guy, and if you're going to bet on something, Cal and that business of his is the way to go," Jake said.

Cal was back and sat across from Grant.

"What do you think?" he asked with clear hope in his voice.

Grant nodded and continued reading through the documents. "This cost analysis looks great. Projected growth is inevitable, and your profit margin is strong." He flipped through the portfolio, then another page. Building log cabins with a modern edge was smart, but the fact that he could expand and make even more money outside Yachats was dollar signs waiting to be cashed.

And Grant knew good business. Which was why Cal had come to him about this opportunity to invest in his company.

"I appreciate you considering investing," Cal said. "I'm good now and loving what I do. But growing bigger might be nice."

"Of course it would," Grant agreed.

"So, you're in New York? Real estate guy? Hannah never really mentioned what you did."

Grant smiled. Because Hannah didn't really know. Still, this question got all the guys' attention; they were looking at him, waiting for an answer.

"I oversee several kinds of businesses. A lot in real estate, and yes, New York is home and where my company is."

As if the devil herself was listening, his phone buzzed in his pocket. Grant glanced at it—it was his mother calling for the eleventh time in twenty-four hours.

"You can design these rustic-looking places with modern features . . . ever consider business establishments instead of homes?" Grant asked.

Cal smiled. "I have. Got some plans written up for a few ideas. Restaurants, office buildings."

Gabe smiled at his friend, and Jake gave him a slap on the back. The men really were friends and supported one another.

Grant nodded at Cal. He'd meant it when they discussed his interest in Cal's company. He had a lot of ideas, all with positive outcomes. It was a matter of making all the moving parts come together, though.

"What's completed down at the subdivision?" he asked Cal.

"The pool and lounge area, several homes, and the main community center in the center of the property."

"I'd liked to host a get-together in one of your completed spaces. Invite some investors. I have some ideas of taking your designs beyond a subdivision. Are you interested?"

"Hell yes, I am," Cal said.

Gabe and Jake also gave a resounding "Absolutely."

"Good. I'll handle the details, and my assistant will be in touch with you about the plans. Bring me some numbers and designs for various establishments. Restaurants, bars, et cetera."

"Will do!" Cal said.

"And," Grant continued, "I want my involvement in this to be between us. I don't want to go telling everyone that I'm looking to expand, including my lovely wife."

He paused to shift his glance between Jake, Cal, and Gabe. They all looked at him with seriousness, and he knew he could trust them. They all nodded.

"Okay," Cal agreed.

"Understood," Gabe and Jake said.

Grant nodded and shook Cal's hand. "Great seeing you," he said as he pulled his cell from his pocket. "I'm sorry to have to ditch out, but I have a few calls I have to make."

"You, too. And thank you."

Grant put his cell to his ear as he walked out of the bar into the sunny afternoon.

"Sarah, I need you to set up a party for me," Grant said to his assistant on the other end of the line. "I'll need Harvey out here."

Grant made a mental note to call his attorney anyway. Harvey oversaw all of Grant's contracts and all aspects of his business. "And this is going to be an investors' meeting, so set up the usual. Get the boys here, and for the details of the party, use Goonies Bar for the bartender and drinks. Pay eight grand for the night and all the liquor. Go local for all the food and decor, as well."

"Yes, sir," Sarah said. "You buying a whole town?"

Grant grinned. "I just may."

He had a lot of plans, all of which he was hoping would make Hannah's life easier . . . especially easier for her to say yes to him at the end of his time here.

Now he just needed to find his wife.

~

"I can't believe you talked me into this," Hannah said to Laura, lighting the last candle in the bar. Several vanilla-scented candles were scattered along the bar top and tables. Tables that were now lining the walls, leaving the bar floor open. Several women with their yoga mats were in the center of the room and facing toward where Laura was stretching. The mighty shark teeth hung on the wall behind her.

Not exactly yoga studio of the year, but it was a large, open space and people had showed up, so Hannah would take what she could get.

"This is a great way to earn that extra money you need," Laura whispered to her. "And you look great!"

Hannah looked at the twenty women who had showed up. Twenty women times twenty bucks was four hundred bucks. Which was something to go toward the money she needed. So she couldn't scoff or be bitchy about it. It was money for her bar. The impromptu yoga class taught by Laura had been—surprise, surprise—Laura's brilliant idea. And because she was wonderful, Laura was teaching the class for free and donating all the money to Hannah's payment.

"Yoga Jäger Night is a new hit!" Laura said. Each woman got a shot of Jägermeister after the hour-long class. The idea of combining alcohol and exercising was the only contribution Hannah had made to this brainchild. But it got attention, so once again, she'd take what she could get. And Laura's stepmom—of sorts—had showed up with the old biddies from downtown.

"Look at you skinny girls!" Roberta said, her massive boobs swaying in her matching neon-pink tank top and stretch pants. She pulled Laura in for a hug, then Hannah. "You both need to come over to the house more, and I'll cook a real meal for you."

"I know you would. All my dad talks about is your cooking," Laura said with a smile.

"Well, I'm just so excited about this little drinking-and-stretching gathering. My smutty readers' club was getting antsy for a new outing. You should host this every week!" Roberta said.

Hannah smiled. "Sounds like a good idea."

Too bad she needed the money in a week. But maybe Hannah would enact permanent Yoga Jäger sessions once she owned the place. Especially since Roberta was the nicest woman in town, and also happened to have the biggest mouth. News, gossip, and every other topic imaginable that passed through town went through Roberta first. And she'd brought four women with her. So maybe this was a good idea long term.

Hannah just had to get to long term first.

"I'm glad you all came," she said, patting Roberta's shoulder. She turned her focus to Laura. "Well, I'll be in the back if you need me."

"Um, no way. You're taking my class, too. Those pants are made for stretching, and that's just what they'll do."

Hannah rolled her eyes. The tank and yoga pants were one thing, but stretching in public? Well, in her bar . . .

"Shoot me now," Hannah mumbled. But she did appreciate her friend helping her, and this little event was bringing in the dough. A few more classes over the next week would get her around a thousand bucks. Four more to go.

"You can't ditch out on class in your own bar," Laura pressed.

"All right," Hannah gave in.

"Here, I brought an extra mat for you," Laura said, handing the rolled-up purple foam mat to Hannah.

"Fantastic."

Hannah gripped the thing and headed to the opposite end of the bar. She was dead last behind everyone and right by the shadowy front-door corner. That way no one could really see her and she could make a quick break for it if she had to.

Because she didn't exactly know what yoga was, since she'd never taken it. But she was pretty sure it had something to do with a dog or a pissed-off baby. Or was it a happy baby?

She shook her head and unrolled her mat, hoping the hour would pass quickly and she could get to her shot of Jäger.

Laura turned off the lights, leaving the place even darker, a soft glow from the candles the only illumination.

"Thank you, everyone, for coming," Laura said, taking her place at the front of the room. "We're going to start with some basic yoga moves today . . ." Her voice was in an oddly soft hippie tone; Hannah just shrugged and tried to follow along.

Hannah took a deep breath, trying to follow the flow of what everyone else seemed to be doing. On a heavy exhale, she bent over into whatever the hell a downward-facing dog was.

∽

Nothing could have prepared Grant for what he walked in on.

His wife, bending over in tight pants.

The bar had been dark, almost glowing, so he'd opened the door quietly, and that's when he'd seen the sign posted on the door.

Yoga and Jäger today!

Smiling at his wife's ingenuity, he walked quietly into the bar, noticing no one was facing him. Thankfully, Hannah was in the dark corner in the back of the group and stretching like he'd never seen a woman move before. Between the shadows and the low music and everyone facing forward, he sneaked behind Hannah as she went into downward-facing dog—and couldn't help but put his hands on her hips.

Her breath hitched, but she didn't pop up. She simply stayed in position and glanced behind her.

"Is that a banana in your pocket, or are you just happy to see me?" she whispered.

Grant smiled. "All happiness, baby."

He gripped her hips and rubbed against her a little. She didn't seem to mind. In fact, her perfect ass pressed into his now growing erection.

"Every damn thing you do is sexy," he said softly in her ear.

"Well, bending over is a little presumptuous."

"Can I take you home and bend you over the couch again?" he asked.

On a deep breath, she moved and shifted her stance, trying to keep up with the flow of the group. Grant was sorry for the loss of her ass against him.

But she reached behind him and ran a hand over his denim-clad cock, and he had to stop himself from moaning.

"Is that your way of asking me on a date?" she said. "Couch banging?"

"That's my way of asking you for anything you'll give me," he said honestly. Not caring how wrapped around her finger he was. He wanted her happy. For her to have everything she wanted. He also wanted her to want him.

Love him.

"Well, I think we can make something work," she said. "But I have to stay here for a while. This stunt of Laura's is bringing in extra money, so I have to pour Jäger shots after this class."

Grant smiled. His wife was an entrepreneur, and it was a sexy side of her. Almost as sexy as her bending over in tight pants.

"Okay, I'll see you later, then."

"Going to stop into a bar twice in one day?" Hannah asked, glancing behind her again to meet Grant's eyes. "Sounds like you have an addiction."

"Absolutely I do," he said.

And he did. Hannah was working late, then he'd be back to see her. "I'll pick you up and give you a ride home."

"That's not necessary," she said.

"I insist."

With a final look at his beautiful wife bending over, he quietly let himself out and started counting the hours until he could have her all to himself. Preferably for an eternity.

∽

"Are you sure this is safe?" Hannah asked, clutching Grant's hand, arm, butt, and then his arm again . . . then back to his butt. She followed in his steps as they climbed up the jagged gray rocks alongside a flowing river.

"I'll keep you safe, baby," he said, glancing over his shoulder to toss her a wink and do a little grabbing of his own. Fire spread from her breasts to her toes as she continued to follow him up and up and up. The warm rock against her bare feet was soothing, despite the climb, and she liked how Grant kept glancing back extra-long at her body, which was on display in a red bikini top and a pair of cutoff shorts.

She wasn't minding the view, either . . .

Grant's perfect ass in a pair of blue swim trunks and tan skin pulled tight over chiseled shoulder muscles.

"I can feel you ogling me, Miss Hastings," he said with a laugh in his voice.

"I'm not sorry," she said.

"Neither am I." He smiled back at her.

Hannah's whole heart fluttered. In fact, it had been doing that same weird flutter thing for the past week. Ever since she'd met Grant. They'd been inseparable.

They'd docked in Jamaica an hour ago and had a whole day to explore before having to get back on the ship to hit the next destination. Nice thing about cruise ships—you could drink and have fun while sailing the sea, then have entire days to explore every port where they docked.

"This is incredible," Hannah said, looking around as she hiked behind Grant along the river and up a mountain. The small group they'd been with had stopped their hike at the last jump point. This beautiful blue river cut through the mountain, stacking slow-flowing waterfalls on top of one another with deep pools at the bottom of each.

The sounds of "Woo-hoo!" and "Yeah!" were echoing from the others who'd decided to jump from one platform down. But Grant wanted to go just a little higher. One more waterfall up. One more pool.

"We're here, baby." He grabbed her hand and helped steady her as they made their way to the edge of the waterfall and looked down at the fifteen-foot drop into crystal-clear water.

She looked down, then out. She was standing in a place she'd never guessed she'd be. In the middle of the beautiful Jamaican countryside, at the edge of a waterfall, with the man she loved.

Her eyes snapped to Grant at the realization her brain kicked out.

"Something wrong?" he asked. His arm snaking around her waist, he looked down at her with concern in his eyes.

"Yeah . . . something is wrong . . . ," she said. She looked into his dark eyes, the high Jamaican sun haloing him, and she couldn't hold back everything her brain and her heart were screaming. "I love you," she admitted.

Grant just looked at her with such easy softness. As if he wasn't surprised, but rather, grateful.

He cupped her face in his hands and kissed her softly on the lips.

"Hannah," he whispered against her mouth. "I want you forever."

A dose of heat and shock surged through her like the antidote to poison. She leaned back and looked him in the eyes. She opened her mouth to say, "What?" or "Are you serious?" but Grant just smiled.

With her face still in his hands, he repeated, "Forever."

A sting hit behind her eyes. She'd never felt this kind of intensity before. The intensity of needing someone. Wanting to need someone.

"Yes," she breathed.

He kissed her hard, and she smiled against his lips.

"Ready to jump?" he said, holding her hand, both of them facing the edge, the unknown, the beauty.

"With you?" She squeezed his hand. "Absolutely."

With that, they jumped off the edge together.

Chapter Seven

Hannah pushed the shopping cart and glanced at Grant, walking next to her.

"You look like you've never gone grocery shopping before," she said, watching him examine the off-brand box of macaroni and cheese for a weirdly long time.

"I live in New York, baby. I usually grab a quick bite out."

"So you never cook?" she asked.

He shook his head. "I can't remember the last time I cooked."

She raised a brow and filed that fact away for later.

He looked good, tall and built with lean muscle, and even his dark blue jeans were made perfectly for his butt. She didn't know if he was trying to dress a bit more casually for her or because he was in a small town, but she liked it. She also loved the blue suit pants he wore with a button-down. Okay, she loved everything he wore, because the man was sexy has hell.

"Something making your mouth water, baby?" he asked and winked at her.

Damn. He'd caught her ogling him. Again. She'd been doing it more and more since he'd been, well, in front of her. That's the problem about Grant being around. She was starting to enjoy him.

"Well, I am hungry and you don't cook, so you're starting to look like a big pork chop." She pushed her cart down the next aisle, slowly going through the frozen food selection.

"Well, I can't have you hungry," he said, coming up behind her and putting his arms around her waist. "I'm very hungry myself and have a taste for . . ." He dipped his hand into the front of her jeans.

"Grant," she said in a hushed tone. His fingers toyed on the outside of her panties against her clit.

There was only one person at the other end of the aisle. Hannah kept walking and wiggled to try to get him to stop—to keep going? She couldn't tell. Couldn't think. She only felt his fingers. He kept his hands discreetly on her while walking behind her.

She was getting hot, bothered, and a whole lot of needy.

Something caught her eye in the frozen case, and she moved to open the door. Grant gently slipped his hand away from her as she got a small carton of vanilla ice cream out of the case.

"Dessert before dinner?" he asked. "I like where your mind is at."

Hannah smiled, then caught of glimpse of something not as good as ice cream.

Her father.

He walked into the grocery store and headed her way.

"Hey, can you go get strawberries and whipped cream? We'll make sundaes," she said to Grant, guiding him down the other end of the aisle.

"Of course. I'll meet you at the checkout."

"Great," she said. Once he rounded the corner, her father was five feet away.

"I saw your car in the parking lot," he said.

Figured.

"What do you need?" she asked.

"Just a few bucks," he said with no shame. They were well past small talk. A few years ago, he would've still tried to hide the fact he needed money by stalling for a sentence or two. Opening the request with phrases like "Weather was good today," or "You still at Goonies?" Now, he got straight to the point, which Hannah appreciated on some level. No sense in trying to pretend there was more to their relationship than there was.

"For food?" she asked, knowing the answer. One of these days she was hoping her father would genuinely need something more than a few bucks for booze. Or to bail him out of whatever mess he was in because he bought booze with his bill money.

"Yes, I need cash for food," he said. Lie. She could tell right away. Her father wasn't exactly elusive when it came to his fibbing. And as always, he wanted cash. Not that Hannah was in the business of writing him checks, but the way he always said the word made every transaction send tremors up her spine.

She looked him in the eye, and he glanced away. He was struggling with his health. The yellow tint to his skin was an obvious sign, not to mention the smell of stale beer and tobacco always wafting off him. Some things never changed, and her father's scent was one of them. He was thin, yet his belly protruded like he was a starving child—or a fifty-plus-year-old man who drank every meal.

"You really need to eat something," she said. She grabbed the small bag of white potatoes and chicken strips she'd already paid for at the deli and handed it to him.

"Thanks," he said, taking it and digging into it right away. "I still could use a few bucks." She opened her mouth to tell him she wasn't giving him money to spend on alcohol, but she saw Grant coming back, strawberries and whipped cream in hand.

Hannah quickly dug ten bucks out of her pocket and handed it to him. She wasn't ready for Grant to meet her father, and she definitely wasn't ready for a scene. Deep down, she knew that her father had no shame and even less pride. If he figured out Hannah was with Grant, he'd hit him up for money, too. And Grant, being the man he was, would give it in a heartbeat.

Nope, none of that was going to happen on her watch. There was no reason Grant needed to meet her dad ever. Hannah only saw him when he needed help or money or bail. And that was how it'd stay.

Silas put the piece of chicken in his mouth and grabbed the money Hannah offered. He didn't say a word. Just continued to chew on another chicken strip and walked away. Toward the exit of the store.

Grant came up to her and put the items in the cart. "Starting to wonder where you were. Who was that?"

"No one," Hannah said, and she honestly felt that way. Every time her father walked away, he left her feeling hollow. Which was strange, because there wasn't much more space to void in her chest. It wasn't that she didn't have a heart—it had just been so beaten up and finally surrounded by steel that she barely felt it beat anymore. Until she was around Grant, that was.

"You okay?" Grant asked, searching her face.

"Yep, excited to get home and eat." She started pushing her cart, and Grant was right there, his warm hand on the small of her back. And for the first time, she didn't feel as ditched as she usually did whenever her father blew in and out of her life.

～

Something had shifted in Hannah at the store. But she wasn't talking about it, which meant Grant would have to try to get some sort of information out of her without coming out and asking.

"Thank you for dinner," he said.

She frowned. "We went to the grocery store only to order pizza."

"Yeah, and it's awesome. Grocery shopping is exhausting. I can't imagine anyone preparing a meal after the effort it takes to acquire the food in the first place."

She smiled and took another bite of pizza. The open box was in the middle of the living room coffee table, and Hannah sat next to Grant on the couch, her legs crossed.

"Now look who's staring," she said.

Grant just shrugged and took a bite of his pizza. "You're nice to look at. I especially like these." He tugged her pajama pants. The thin, soft material had pink cartoon moose on them. Her white tank top was sexy, especially since she wasn't wearing a bra.

"These are my comfy hang-out clothes."

"Well, I'm in full support of them."

She laughed. "How do you do that?"

"Do what?"

She put her pizza down and looked at him. "Make me feel pretty even in this." She motioned to her outfit.

Wait, was she serious? Because the woman was gorgeous all the time. In any clothing. Though he preferred her in none. And she really didn't feel pretty before?

Part of him wanted to feel good that he made her feel that way; the other part wanted to grill her on why the hell she didn't feel beautiful all the time. It was so clear to him how incredible she was.

He ran his finger along her cheekbone and leaned in to kiss her softly.

Her eyelashes fluttered against his cheek, and he'd never loved the feeling of anything so much in his life.

She felt delicate. But he knew she was strong willed. In this moment, she was his.

She kissed him back, her sweet lips parting, and she slowly grabbed the hem of his T-shirt and lifted it up over his head. Her hands came down and ran the length of him. He loved the feel of her touch against his skin. Wanting him. Learning him.

He wanted to be everything she wanted.

Her lips grazed down his jaw to his neck, then down to his chest.

He wanted to tunnel his hands in her silky hair, but he didn't want to dictate this moment. He wanted her to do whatever she wanted. And he was interested to see where she'd take this.

Her lips kissed along his nipple, and she was soft in every lick and sweep of her hands. It was driving him insane. He wanted more. Deeper, harder, rougher. To reach out and toss her over the couch and take her. To hug her close and wrap every inch of himself around her.

Make her take it.

Make her love it.

Make her love *him*.

Instead, he kept his willpower. Kept his hands to himself. Let her kiss him. Because the feeling of her mouth on his skin was incredible.

It wasn't until he heard the jingle of his belt being unfastened that he realized she was trying to tug his pants off. He adjusted enough to let her have access. His jeans hit the floor, and he sat there in his boxer briefs, his woman kissing him.

Her soft hands then started to peel back his underwear. Trailing them down his legs and off, while her mouth grazed his belly button. He was hard and hot and ready, and she went slow with her soft touches.

"Stay right here. Don't move," she whispered, then got up quickly and left the room.

What the hell? He felt like an idiot sitting there, but he did as she asked. She came back into view and placed the strawberries, whipped cream, and ice cream on the coffee table.

"I want to try something," she said and knelt in front of him. She was holding a spoon, her cute little pants and amazing breasts on display for him.

Grant had a chill just watching her open the small carton so close to his lap.

"Calm down, I'm not going to freeze your dick off," she said with a smile.

Grant laughed. "I'm all yours, baby. Just trying to figure out what you're doing."

"I heard about this trick . . . ," she started, dipping the spoon into the ice cream and taking a bite. Grant watched, transfixed. The most beautiful woman he'd ever seen was kneeling before him, between his spread knees, eating ice cream.

If this was a dream, he didn't want to wake up.

"Apparently, there are different sensations to be had," she said, taking another bite of ice cream, letting the spoon slowly slip from her lips. Grant was hard and ready to experience whatever these sensations were.

She took another bite of ice cream, then, with it still in her mouth, she bent forward. With her lips an inch from his raging hard-on, she exhaled slowly, her cool vanilla breath hitting the tip. Shivers raced up his spine, but his cock grew hotter and harder.

"Jesus," he mumbled, trying to figure out where his brain was going.

He watched her throat bob on a swallow, then she snaked her tongue out and licked the crown.

"Oh my God," he said and gripped the couch at his sides. Her tongue was cold, and it buzzed against his hot skin. He'd never felt anything like it.

"Not too bad, right?" she asked with a sexy smile.

"There's nothing bad about what you're doing," he confirmed and once again checked the urge to cup her face and thrust himself deep into her throat. Grant was used to hard and rough, and Hannah seemed to like that. Asked him for it. But at this moment, the teasing and slow torture got him turned on in a way he never had been.

Delayed gratification had never been a part of his vocabulary, but he was seeing the upside to it. Because he was the luckiest son of bitch alive to have this woman see to him like she was. He wouldn't do anything to interrupt her.

"This is your show, baby," he said around a ragged breath.

She kissed around his navel, his hard cock bobbing against her neck, as if begging for attention. His fists squeezed the couch cushions harder.

She took another bite of ice cream, and when she came back, it was still in her mouth.

With an eyebrow raised and a saucy grin, she took him into her mouth, sucking hard. The cool vanilla swirled around his cock as she sucked up and down. The feel of her mouth, mixed with the cool cream sliding in and out of her throat, was the best damn thing he'd ever felt.

"Jesus, baby, you have me close already." It was embarrassing, actually, how quickly she could get him to come. He'd never wanted someone so badly in his life, and he was already on the brink. Which he wouldn't allow, since he hadn't even gotten a chance to taste Hannah, or even get her close.

She hummed around him, swallowing while she still took him into her mouth, and Grant's eyes rolled to the back of his head. Wait. He needed her. Needed to taste her. Feel her. He wasn't ready for this to be over yet, and he wanted to play this game, too.

"My turn," he said, his voice hoarse from trying to keep his composure.

Hannah sat back and looked at him.

"Don't you like what I'm doing?" she asked.

"Baby, I love it. But I want a turn. Not very fair that I don't get to eat you," he said with a wink. Her eyes went heavy, and he knew she was interested in what he had to offer.

He peeled her tank top off, then had her stand up. He tugged her pants down, kissing her hips and down her thighs as he went. Her hands tunneled in his hair, and he loved the feeling of her holding on to him.

He slowly shifted to have her sit on the couch, so he was now the one kneeling in front of her. Gripping the backs of her knees, he slid her down just a little and spread her legs.

"If I had known dining in would be this fun, I would have never left my house," Grant said, staring down at his beautiful wife. He forced himself to take his time and not fall on her, ravaging her like a damn animal.

He reached for the ice cream and spread it on her nipple with a finger. She gasped, and the pebbled peak budded harder. He sucked her hard. Cleaning the vanilla off her and laving at her skin.

"That feels amazing," she breathed. And Grant understood, having had the cold and hot sensations from her just a moment ago.

Starting at her small waist, he rubbed down her body, his thumbs skimming over her hips, massaging gently as he went. She arched into him, her eyes fluttering closed as if she were relaxed and loving his touch. He sure as hell hoped so, because the woman had him spinning and ready to beg.

Kissing her belly button, he reached behind him and grabbed the whipped cream and shook it.

"Hold still," he said and placed the edge of the nozzle near her clit. He sprayed a large helping of cream, and she giggled and squirmed. Her entire center was covered, and he placed the can back on the coffee table and took out a strawberry.

"You still hungry?" he asked. "Because I'm starving."

He swiped the strawberry in the cream between her legs and took a bite.

"You are the most delicious thing I've ever tasted," he said, going in for another sample.

She moved her hips out, as if wanting more. Grant knew she loved it when he went deep. Loved it when he was hard and rough. But she'd teased him, so fair was fair.

He licked at some of the cream between her legs, purposefully glossing over her most sensitive spot, and watched her squirm and beg for more.

"Please, you're right there . . . ," she breathed, her eyes closing and her lithe body trying to tempt him to take her further.

"Right where?" he asked. "Right here . . . ?" He gave a hard lick to her clit, the cream melting around her.

"Yes!" she said.

With a grin, he stiffened his tongue and thrust it inside her. The taste of cream and her pleasure hit his mouth, and he was desperate for more.

He thrust in and out. Drinking her down and loving the flavor.

"Please, please, Grant." Her hands gripped his hair. "Please, I need more. Take me hard. Please."

He couldn't deny her pleas. And he couldn't deny his need for her, either. He rose up on his knees and grabbed her hips, pulling her spread legs open and toward him, impaling her on his cock in one yank.

"Oh God! Yes," she screamed.

Grant groaned at her hot sheath surrounding him. He pumped in and out of her. The cream sliding around them only spurred him on.

She pushed his chest, causing him to fall back on the carpet. She followed him down, still fastened to him, and started riding him.

"Jesus, baby, you're the best," he groaned. He gripped her hips and worked her up and down on his cock. Her hands dug into his chest while she moved on him. Her breasts bounced, and Grant leaned up enough to snag a nipple in his mouth and give a quick suck. Then a little bite to the other.

She gasped his name and rode him harder. Faster. Taking him deep, then moving her hips back and forth. He could feel himself hitting that spot inside she loved so much. He watched her eyes squeeze shut as she threw her hips back and forth, seeking her own pleasure. Using him to find it.

It was the most incredible sight Grant had ever seen.

He loved having his control. Taking charge. But lying there, watching his woman use him to get herself off, was the sexiest thing he'd

SA MA 4012
Expires: Friday, 25 September 2020
39090038887945
Please check out this item

SA AM 4072

2020 September 25, Friday : Expires

3608003886945

please check out this item

witnessed. And he wanted to be whatever she needed. Even if that meant giving her control in this moment.

"Come on, baby," he urged her on. "Come on me. I want to feel it."

He flexed his hips just enough to hit her just a little deeper, and she threw her head back on a moan. So he did it again. And once more.

"Oh God, I'm coming," she cried. Her long hair grazed the tops of his thighs, and she cried his name to the ceiling. Her hot core squeezing and milking him as he felt her orgasm lit up his entire body.

It was her pleasure that sent him over the edge.

"Baby, I'm there."

She grounded down on him, rocking hard and taking him through his own release. Buried deep inside her, he came hard. Sparks lit up from the base of his spine and spread to his limbs like wildfire.

She collapsed on top of him, breathing hard and kissing his chest.

He wrapped his arms around her, and they stayed like that for a long moment. Feeling her heart beat against his, her mouth on his skin, her hair covering them like a blanket, he'd never felt more complete. He also felt like the whole world was lying in his arms, and at some point, he'd have to let it go.

But not tonight.

Not this week.

Keeping her against him, he sat up, then made it to his feet. Carrying his wife to the bedroom, he gently laid her down and settled her in bed. She was half-asleep and smiling, and Grant went to get a warm washcloth to clean the sticky cream off her.

She was still smiling with her eyes closed, and Grant could have sworn he heard her mumble his name and the word *love*.

His chest pounded hard at the hope of that.

He brought the blankets to her chin and tucked her in tightly. Her lips parted around even breaths and her hair splayed wild over the pillow. She looked sated, happy, relaxed. And Grant wanted to stay in this moment a little longer. Because it was in this moment that she'd loved on him. He'd loved on her. And now, he was going to share a bed with his wife.

A dream . . . it has to be a dream . . .

And there was no way in hell he'd let himself wake up if it meant he got to stay a few more moments in this perfect bliss.

～

Hannah had managed to avoid Grant this morning. Leaving him sleeping while she quietly sneaked out for her doctor's appointment. He was getting to her, and she was admitting more than she'd ever thought she would. So much that she was forgetting that his time in Yachats was dwindling, and once he was gone, he'd be gone.

That was the deal.

So why wasn't that fact bringing her relief?

Her stomach twisted, and she crossed, then uncrossed her legs in the waiting room chair, preparing for another long day.

"You nervous?" Laura asked her from the seat next to her. The doctor's office smelled clean and crisp. Early-morning appointments worked easiest for Hannah, since the bar didn't open until lunchtime.

"No, I'm fine. This is routine." Hannah tried to convince herself that she really was fine, but deep down, she wasn't. "You know, you don't still have to come with me to these appointments."

"Aside from my absence, when I lived in California, I've been coming to these with you since we were freshmen in high school." Laura smiled and patted Hannah's hand. Hannah had been fine going to these appointments by herself when Laura was gone, but Laura seemed to have some guilt, so Hannah indulged her.

She wished she had a better reason for needing a doctor. Truth was, Hannah was annoyed by the situation. Since the doctor had found cysts on her ovaries when she was fourteen, over the years the message had turned from "no big deal" to "we should monitor these," with hushed talk that Hannah might be barren.

"Everything will be okay," Laura said, like she said every six months when she came to her appointment with her.

"Yeah, it will. Because worst case, my parts don't work and they take them out. No big deal."

Laura frowned at her. "Hannah, it is a big deal. The cysts are okay now, but if they turned into something . . ." She paused, trying to stay positive. "I don't want you to lose your parts," she said, mimicking Hannah's language.

"It's not like I'd die," Hannah countered. "I just couldn't have kids. So what."

Laura let out a deep exhale. "That's a big deal."

"I don't even want kids, so it's really not," Hannah said. She glanced away and saw *Parenting* magazine on the small side table, with a rosy-cheeked baby staring back at her. She wondered what Grant's baby would look like. Beautiful, of course. With his eyes and smile and—

Why the hell am I thinking about babies? Stop it.

"You'd be a good mom," Laura said softly, tapping into the major fear Hannah had.

No . . . I wouldn't be.

She was a product of her mother—a woman who'd left her child—and her father, a drunk who didn't give a shit about his child. Hannah didn't have the DNA to be a parent, and she would never put an innocent child through her bumbling attempts at parenting. Because the single most terrifying question pierced her brain every time she started to wonder about having a child . . .

Would I be just like my father?

The fear was too real and way too scary to risk.

"And Grant seems like a great guy and—"

"I'm not having a baby with Grant," Hannah cut her friend off.

Laura shrugged. "You're married to him. You've never discussed a family?"

"We eloped on a cruise ship," Hannah said with exasperation.

"You love him, though. You're married to him. He brings out the best in you."

Hannah frowned. Laura's own brows were knit. She was assertive and serious.

"What are you giving me a hard time on this?" Hannah asked.

"I'm not, I just want you to try thinking through other options. Stop running from the good things."

Hannah shook her head. "I'm not ready for a baby, and I don't even know that my marriage will work out."

"I'm not saying go have a baby, I'm saying that you should at least talk to the man you love and open up about what you feel. What you're afraid of."

Hannah huffed out a breath, trying to get this gut-wrenching pain to leave her stomach. With every breath it just twisted deeper. The ache pulsed upward until it beat in her throat like a drum.

She thought of Grant. Of all the other times she'd been consumed by this . . . fear. How he soothed her.

Last night had been incredible. After they'd had their dessert, Grant had cleaned her up and tucked her in bed. She'd slept hard. Feeling lost to happy exhaustion and secure with Grant's warm body next to hers.

When she'd woken up this morning, she'd caught sight of his cell phone blinking. A text was displayed from some guy named Harvey, wishing Grant a happy birthday tomorrow. She realized that she was finding out little facts about Grant that she hadn't known. Like that he had a birthday coming up. She'd focus on that. Focus on the time she had with Grant and not worry about all this other crap. Like the future. Or the all-important discussion one was apparently supposed to have with one's spouse. Jesus, Hannah couldn't even elope right. Had no idea how to be married or what came with it. Much less how to have a discussion about more.

"I need to buy my bar. I need a business, stability. That is my baby," Hannah said to Laura, shutting down the conversation. She needed to get her mind right and stay focused on what she did have control over.

The nurse called for Hannah, and she got up and walked back. This conversation was over.

∼

The doctor's appointment turned out like any other. Monitor and watch and hope. Whatever. Hannah was happy to be at work with her mind busy on the tasks of running the bar. The bar phone rang, and Hannah spun to grab it.

"Goonies Bar, this is Hannah."

"Hi, this is Sarah Roth. I am interested in your services for an event. May I speak to the manager?"

Hannah frowned and held the phone away from her ear enough to glance at it. Not that she'd see a damn thing. But the call was unprecedented. Not to mention the term *manager* likely would be applied to Hannah, if her boss thought titles were ever necessary. Hannah would be the one to speak to in this situation. Plus, she was hell-bent on owning this bar, so either way . . . she could handle this.

"This is the manager," Hannah finally said.

"There is an event being hosted at the new subdivision next Friday, at the Cal James Cabins ranch house. We'd like you to provide bartending services for the event."

Hannah knew exactly where that was. That was the place Cal was working on, and everyone had their eye on these new homes going in.

"Okay, how long are you needing a bartender?"

"The entire evening, roughly six p.m. until eleven. You provide your own liquor, and the flat rate is eight thousand for the night. Are you interested?"

Ah, fuck yeah, she was! That was her goal for what she needed to make the balloon payment minus alcohol cost. She couldn't believe that she would actually make this work. With this one side job, she'd finally have her bar.

"Yes, I can do that," Hannah said, trying not to sound overly crazy with excitement.

"Wonderful. I will need your e-mail address to send all the details and the mailing address on where to send the funds," Sarah said. The confident, routine tone of her voice made Hannah think she'd booked these kind of events a hundred times before. But this one was the gateway to changing Hannah's life.

Hannah gave Sarah all her contact information and thanked her before hanging up. She smiled so wide it hurt her face. If this event came through, she'd be able to pay for the bar and it would actually be hers.

Hope and happiness raced through her, and she almost couldn't believe it. She knew better than to count on anything until the money was in hand, but this should work out!

She bounced on her toes, thinking of all the fun things she wanted to get done today. One being do something special for Grant's birthday tomorrow. He didn't know that she knew, but she wanted to at least acknowledge his big day.

She pursed her lips and tried to think of what she could do for him . . . get him . . .

Her day was looking up. That was, until her least favorite customer came in—her father.

"You know I won't serve you," she said to him.

He ignored her and sat at the bar anyway. "I came to see my little girl," he said.

Hannah looked him over. Wasn't the worst she'd ever seen him, but not the best. His jeans were dirty, and his white T-shirt was wrinkled and stained with either a few drops of blood or barbecue sauce. It was then she noticed he was missing one of his upper teeth.

Guess it was blood.

And she didn't want to know any more. It was equally likely that her father had gotten in a fight, fallen, or ripped his own tooth out on a wager. In all cases, she'd rather not know.

He scratched his knuckles along his cheek, the gray stubble making a sandpaper noise as he did. He looked tired. Dark circles around his eyes and splotchy, leathery skin. He was fifty-five and looked closer to seventy. There were more sunspots on the top of his balding head, and Hannah wondered if she should take him to the doctor to get those checked out.

"What do you need?" she asked.

"Just came to see my girl," he said. She wasn't sure why he returned to small talk. Maybe he was drunk already? Maybe he was gearing up to ask for something other than money? A flare of hope pierced her ribs.

"What is it, Silas?"

He smiled, then frowned, then sighed. A ping of worry raced up her spine like an eel on speed.

That eel instantly died when it hit the back of her neck.

"Rent is due," he spit out. So it really was just about money. Stupid she'd think otherwise, even for a moment. Why was she surprised? The fact that she kept giving it to him said, if anything, how stupid she was. Granted, she tried not to look at it that way. If her father didn't pay rent, he'd be homeless. Because no way in hell would she take him in, and there was literally nowhere else for him to go. So keeping him in a roof and walls was good for Hannah, her father, and society in general.

She'd been a pawn in her dad's game long enough to know her way around the con.

"Rent is three fifty a month," she said. For a trailer out in the middle of nowhere, you got what you pay for.

He nodded. "I'm short two hundred."

"Okay," she said with a solid breath and placed her hands on the bar top. "I'll pay the two hundred to your landlord."

He laughed. The raspy, sleepy laugh of a man who was used to having an esophagus full of whiskey.

"Just give it to me, and I'll run it over right now."

Now Hannah laughed. "Never."

He raised a brow. "Fine. Don't trust your dad. That says more about your character than mine."

"Don't start with me about character," she said, realizing how low her tone had gotten on those last words.

"I can say whatever I want," he spat. "You're the daughter who runs a bar with an alcoholic father. Like you want to kill me while laughing."

"At least you admit that you're an alcoholic," she said.

He slammed his hand down. "You always were ungrateful."

"Time for you to go," she said. Because her father was the only person in the world who scared her. He was frail, likely drunk, and still, the hatred in his voice hit a chord deep in her soul. That same chord that gave her a healthy dose of realization that people couldn't be counted on and they ended up hurting you.

"Out," she said, hating that her voice was a whisper.

He shook his head, looking genuinely disappointed in her. An invisible knife twisted through Hannah's heart. She shouldn't care. But the way her father just stared at her—like he really was embarrassed, annoyed, and put out—made her heart sink.

She watched him stumble away. He was looking sickly. So old and frail, and she didn't want to know how bad off his body was. And yet she knew her father wouldn't live to see sixty-five. Which gave her just a few years. There was no proof of any of this, but there was proof she was an idiot, because deep down, she cared. And she was worried she always would.

Chapter Eight

Hannah sat quietly across a white linen–covered table from Grant. She looked lovely but said almost nothing. Like her mind was racing. And Grant would give just about anything to know what the woman thought of. What troubled her. What she loved.

He'd spent more time with Jake. Between taking calls and working remotely by e-mail, he found Jake becoming a good friend, and grabbing a beer to shoot the shit before Hannah got home was nice. Grant had never had a real friend before.

Jake talked about his life, his wife, the future. Every topic garnered a wide smile while he discussed the woman he loved and the future they had. Made Grant think about Hannah. Well, he always thought about Hannah, but being around another man he respected who was married and in love made Grant think in different ways.

He'd gone into this ruse with the sole intent of getting Hannah to agree to stay married to him and come to New York. But there was more to his grand plan. Items he'd tackle as they came along, but those items were now at the forefront of his mind, led by one single word:

Future.

There was a lot of life ahead of Grant and Hannah, and he wanted to provide the best for her, and for the family they could have one day. Between the business and their locations, he hadn't thought about the next step beyond simply keeping Hannah. He wanted to talk to her about all this. Wanted to know what she thought about and what she wanted, other than her bar.

"This place is great," Grant said, taking a bite of his pasta. The small Italian restaurant was on the south side of town, in an old seaside house from the early 1900s that had been converted into a restaurant. Cozy and intimate. If only he could get his wife to open up to him.

"Yeah, this is one of my favorite places," Hannah said with a forced smile. She pushed her chicken around on her plate. Grant wanted to come out and ask her to tell him what was on her mind. But he was worried if he pushed too hard, she'd shut down. So he'd try to get her talking without being obvious.

"So you come here a lot?" he asked.

She shook her head. "No, I don't go out often."

"Well, working at Goonies probably gets exhausting. You put in a lot of long hours, baby. You're a hard worker."

She glanced up at him, and a small smile tugged her lips. "Thank you," she said.

He was getting somewhere.

"What was your favorite place to go when you were growing up around here?" he asked.

She frowned at her plate then smiled. "Candy shop."

He laughed and nodded. "I can see why. The whole block smells like taffy."

"Banana is my favorite," she said, taking a bite of her food. Her shoulders squared just a little to show Grant she was coming out of whatever was weighing them down. He wanted to keep going. To make her happy. To watch her perk up in his presence.

"You and Laura go there?" he asked.

Hannah raised a brow at him. "Yes."

He shrugged. "I like thinking about you before we met. You and Laura have been friends for a while. Jake told me the gist."

"Glad to see you're checking up on me."

"Just wanting to know my wife," he said.

Her eyes shot to his. Wasn't a glare, so that was good.

"So you heard about my appointment, then?" she grumbled and followed up with some remark about small-town gossip and how it figured Laura told Jake and Jake told Grant. But Grant had no idea what the hell she was talking about. Before he could ask, Hannah cut him off.

"Well, I want to know you, too. Like, for example, you have a birthday tomorrow."

That surprised Grant. "How could you possibly know that?"

Hannah smiled and took a bite of her food. "I have my ways."

He huffed, his plan backfiring. He wanted to know her, not field questions about his birthday or wonder how his wife was gaining her intel.

"What? You don't like your birthday? Is it because you're old?" she teased.

"I'm not old," he said.

"Older than me," she countered, that sassy, flirty attitude hitting full gear. He loved her when she played with him. "Come on, tell me how old you are."

He glanced at his plate. He knew his wife was twenty-nine, and while he wasn't old, he just didn't do birthdays or celebrating anything that had to do with himself. She was in a better mood, though, so he'd take that as a win.

"Come on," she pressed. "Don't you think it's weird a wife doesn't know how old her husband is?"

"I'm thirty-seven tomorrow."

A small grin split her face.

"What?" he asked.

"Nothing." Her smile got bigger. "Just that I bagged myself a silver fox."

"I don't have gray hair," he said seriously. Because he checked. Every morning.

She laughed. "Well, I'm excited to celebrate your birthday tomorrow."

"No," he said. "Absolutely not."

"Too bad. It's happening."

Grant took a calming breath, because the woman was irritating him again. But in a good way. Still more irritating than good, because he hated celebrating his birthday. It was always stupid parties full of fake people and a thousand dollars a plate. No, he didn't a need a celebration. Then he had an idea . . .

"You want to celebrate my birthday?" he asked.

"Yes," Hannah said, happily chewing her food.

"Then talk to me."

"Ah, I am," she said.

"I mean, really talk to me. Starting with answering a few questions."

"Like my favorite color?"

No, not like your favorite color at all. He wanted real answers to real questions and for her to stop avoiding him and certain topics.

"Just a few honest questions to obtain honest answers," he said.

She pushed food around her plate, not meeting his eyes, and said, "Okay."

Grant swallowed hard. He finally had his wife willing to talk to him. He wanted to dive in and rattle off everything, but he had to go slow. Hope she would stick with him and trust him with what he was seeking. Which was her.

"That man the other night at the grocery store . . . ," he started.

Hannah's shoulders slumped slightly. "That was my father."

"He lives around here?" Grant asked.

"Yep, but he only comes around when he needs something. He's a drunk. Probably sick. His body can't keep up with the crap he's doing."

He nodded. This was clearly painful for her. His strong wife stiffened to stone whenever sadness or fear crept in. He'd seen it before and wished he could take her in his arms and make everything better. He also knew pieces of her life from the hints she'd given in the past and from Jake and Gabe filling in some of the blanks. Grant had been lucky enough to have a wonderful father and couldn't imagine what Hannah had gone through growing up.

"Is that the appointment you had today? Did you take him somewhere because he's sick?"

"No," she said, her voice soft. "I have tried taking him to the doctor in the past, but he refuses. The appointment was mine. I thought you knew through the Laura–Jake grapevine."

Grant shook his head. "No, I didn't know." He wished he did. Wished he was a part of her every day and knew every moment. "Are you okay?"

"Yeah, it's just a semiannual thing I've had to go to since I was in high school. No big deal."

"If it's no big deal, then what is it?"

She took another bite and shrugged off her own words before she even spoke them. "They just check my ovaries, making sure they're okay and these spots on them continue to be okay."

Blood drained from Grant's face, and his heart sputtered.

"Grant." She reached across the table and grabbed his hand. "I'm really okay. This is why I get checked."

He nodded but felt like someone had just punched him in the gut. "You swear to me you're okay?"

"I swear." She looked over his face, and he wanted to know more. Needed her to be okay. He'd never thought for a second she wasn't or wouldn't always be.

She leaned back and returned to her food, something clearly going through her mind.

"What?" he asked.

She met his stare again. "Do you think about having kids?"

Her question physically pushed Grant back in his chair. That was out of the blue, yet, he could see how it'd be relevant, since Grant had recently been thinking similar things. The future, family, kids . . . he could understand, and honestly, he wanted to get her thoughts on this as well. It was a good sign she was asking and thinking about the future.

"Yes," he said honestly. "I think about the future and having kids."

"So you want them?"

"Yes. I never thought about it much before, but I know it's something I've always wanted. Having a son to pass down—" He cut himself off from saying anything about his father's business—now his business. "I want to pass down the kind of man my father was to my son." That was honest, and Grant really did want to pass that, and even more, down to his children.

"A son, huh? What, girls aren't good enough?"

"I didn't mean that. I'd want a girl. I'd love a girl, especially if she's like you." Again, the most honest thing he felt. Hannah's gaze met his, and there was a sadness behind those eyes. "I'm an only child and was raised mostly by my dad, so my brain goes straight to 'son,' but I wouldn't care if we had a dozen little girls, because with you as their mom, they'd be strong and proud and gorgeous."

Her lips parted, her brows knitting together like she'd been slapped. What had he said to make her look like that? Like he'd caused her pain.

"Do you not want kids?" he asked.

She glanced away. "No, I don't."

Grant was confused, and for a moment, he thought he'd misheard her. "Are you kidding?" he asked.

"No. Why would I joke about that?"

"I don't know, I just figured . . ."

"Grant, our marriage isn't exactly stable."

"It's romantic, though," he countered. A flare of red-hot anger flashed in his gut. "We've made progress, and I've been a good sport on letting you keep your pride and pretend our relationship is a joke. But you love me. Stop acting like you don't. And stop acting like our marriage is going to fail."

She set her palms on the table and leaned forward. "I'm not pretending anything. This relationship is tearing me up, and for God's sake, look around you. You're in Yachats, Oregon. You want to give a speech about pretending? Stop acting like this is an easy situation. Stop thinking there's a quick fix to this, because our lives are different. What we want is different."

"Like kids," he snapped back. How could he love this woman and feel like he was losing her at the same time?

"Yes."

"Why?"

"Because I'd be a shitty mom," she said, then covered her mouth. The raw cut in her words seemed to shock even her, and Grant's skin heated while his lungs fogged up, searching for a clean breath.

"Baby, you can't honestly think that."

"Grant, I can't even get married correctly. I got lost on an island, for Christ's sake. I can't even find my shoes half the time, and my job mostly consists of cursing out drunk fishermen. I'm not mother material."

"You're the best kind of mother material." Any baby would be lucky to have Hannah's strength and ambition. She worked hard for everything. Loved even harder. But Hannah was seeing what Grant saw in her, only backward.

"My father is a drunk, and my mother is gone. There's not one shred of DNA in me I'd burden a baby with, and I sure as hell won't pass down whatever mutated awfulness I have running through my blood."

Grant stood up, his chair loudly pushing backward along the floor, and he didn't give a shit who noticed. He walked around the table to Hannah. She spun her chair to face him, and he hit his knees and cupped her face in his hands.

"What are you doing?" she asked.

"Telling you that I love you and you are the best woman in the world and I don't care what it takes—one day, you'll see yourself the way I see you."

He kissed her hard. Her thick eyelashes fluttered over his cheek, like she was blinking fiercely.

"It's my birthday," Grant whispered against her mouth. "Does that mean I get a present?"

"Yes," she whispered.

"Okay, I want my wife."

She leaned back an inch to meet his gaze. "What does that mean?"

"Exactly what I said. I want my wife. Interpret how you will." He gave her a wink and rose. Walking back to his seat, he finished his meal with his wife, determined to never let her go.

~

He said he wanted his wife, Hannah thought as she washed a pan in the sink. Last night at dinner, Grant had actually made her feel better. Any time her father was in the equation, it left her with a bad taste in her mouth.

Then dinner had taken her back. She'd been spinning the notion of kids and the future around in her brain since Laura had mentioned it at her appointment. And Grant apparently thought about those things, too.

Her nerves were still frazzled from the conversation and the realization of how much she doubted herself in the mothering department. It was how Grant looked at her, how he held her, that made her chest crack. Like her heart was trying to break free through her ribs. She didn't know if his faith in her made her feel a little better, or a little sick.

"A little of both," she mumbled to herself.

But Grant had been kind. Seemed genuinely interested in her. Almost willing to take some of the burden of what was going through her mind.

Dare she hope? Having someone be your—what was that word?—oh! *Partner*. That was an odd concept. Hannah had always taken care of everything herself. Even her own parent. She didn't remember a time she felt like someone else was ready and willing to take on life with her.

She scrubbed the pan in circles and thought about tonight.

Thought about everything she had planned for Grant.

She was still very aware that this was over in a week. In fact, she was actually trying not to think of that too hard. Because then she started to have this twinge of pain in her chest. She liked having him around. He bugged the crap out of her and challenged her, but he also soothed her and took over when she needed him to.

"Wife," she whispered out loud. It didn't make her cringe as much as it had. She flicked the garbage disposal on and smiled. It worked perfectly. Because her husband had fixed it.

Husband.

Whoa, time to stop this train of thought. Because at the end of the day, they were just playing. This would end. He lived on the other side of the country. *Unless he moved here . . . ?*

She shook her head. She couldn't get too attached. Could she?

No. Not a good idea. She would take this remaining week because she had no choice. Well, sort of no choice. It wasn't exactly torture, unless she counted what it was doing to her heart. She had missed Grant, and now with him back, she understood why. He made her feel wanted. But what was worse, he made her feel safe. She wasn't alone with him. Wasn't taking on everything by herself.

She glanced around. The house was clean, and she was ready to get Grant's birthday present going. He'd left this morning and would be out all day. He'd told her he had errands and business. Worked for her. She had the day off and the house to herself.

"Operation Honey, I'm Home has commenced."

The sun was setting when Grant walked up to his wife's little home, with the little door, in her little town. He'd done some exploring. Had a few meetings and took calls at the library business center. It wasn't a high-rise in New York, and yet, he liked the cozy feel of his workday. He also needed a reason to stay out, because he didn't want Hannah throwing his birthday in his face all day.

But the best part was that at the end of today, he was going home. To his wife.

Well, it was her home, but it felt like home because she was in it.

He opened the door and heard an upbeat song coming from the stereo. The house was warm and clean and smelled like pork chops.

"Honey, I'm home," he said with a joking smile and set his bag down by the door. He unbuttoned the cuffs of his blue shirt and started rolling them up while he took two steps toward the kitchen—then froze in his tracks at the sight that greeted him.

"Well, look at my big strong man home from a big strong day," Hannah said in a cutesy voice as she walked toward him, carrying a tray of food and wearing nothing but a 1950s-style apron and red high heels.

"Best. Birthday. Ever," he said, watching his gorgeous wife set a plate of pork chops on the table. Her sexy legs in those shoes made him instantly hard. And having a prime view of her breasts that were barely concealed by her apron had him dying to rip it off her.

"You said you wanted a wife as your present, right?" she said, keeping her voice sweet. "Well, birthdays are special around here, and we aim to please, Mr. Laythem."

With a smile, she spun on her heel and headed back to the kitchen. Grant watched her bare, perfect ass strut away.

He was really starting to like this birthday concept.

"Sit down. You must be famished," Hannah said, pulling out his seat. He took it, and she bent over, her breasts an inch from his face as she set a plate of rolls next to him. He couldn't help but snake his tongue out and lick her cleavage. She gave a small gasp then stood up straight.

"Careful, now. We have an entire birthday meal to get through first."

"I want you as my meal," he said.

She smiled. Grant had never seen her like this. Her black hair was pulled up into a neat bun, and her eyes were lined with a charcoal color that made her bright red lips pop.

"Did you get your version of 'wife' from *I Love Lucy*?" he asked.

"Maybe," she said softly.

"I love it," he said with all the seriousness he felt, running a hand up the back of her bare thigh.

"I just put my dirty spin on a 1950s housewife," she said.

Grant's hand slowly met the cleft of her ass. "I really love it."

She smiled again, but there was heat in her eyes and Grant had no interest in dinner. He just wanted to devour the gorgeous woman in front of him.

"I have one more surprise for you," she whispered, then slid away from him and went back to the kitchen. She came out with a small, circular cake, a single candle lit on top of it.

"Happy birthday," she said and held it out. He scooted his chair away from the table and tugged her hips so she stood before him. He had his wife between his legs, holding a cake, and he'd never felt so grateful in his life.

"Make a wish," she said, and he looked at her for a long, long time.

I wish you loved me as much as I love you . . .

He blew out the candle.

She smiled and went to walk back to the kitchen, but he stopped her.

"I need to get a knife and plates for all this," she said.

"Don't go." He took the cake from her hands and set it on the table. "Pink frosting?"

"Strawberry. Your favorite."

He loved that she knew that.

"Thank you for dinner and all your hard work today, wife," he said. He rose and lifted her to sit on the table. "But I think it's time you take a break and relax."

He spread her legs and stepped between them.

"You should have a bite of your cake, at least," she breathed. She reached over and swiped her finger in the strawberry icing and held it to his lips. He sucked her little finger hard and clean and watched her eyes the entire time.

"You're right, baby. That is good." He reached behind her neck and untied the apron and peeled the top down, baring her high, round breasts. "But I was serious when I said I want you for dinner also."

He gently pushed her back so she lay on the table, the best damn offering he'd ever had. He took another swipe of his cake and pasted it over her breasts, coating her from throat to nipples.

She arched and squirmed, and Grant bent over her, running his tongue through the path of the frosting.

"Mmm," he muttered, sucking hard on her nipple, the sweet taste of her skin and strawberries hitting his mouth. "You're delicious."

"You better be careful, because I think you may be getting addicted to sugar," she said. Grant thought back to all the wonderful things he'd eaten off her and couldn't be sorry.

"Oh, I have an addiction, all right," he said, taking another taste of her frosted nipple while unbuttoning his pants and shoving them low on his hips. He climbed up on the table, hovering over her. "Tell me you want me."

"I want you," she whispered.

He let his body rest only an inch above hers. His cock prodded her opening.

"Tell me how you want me," he asked.

Looking up at him, she brushed her mouth against his and said, "Hard."

That was all Grant needed. He reached behind her head and gripped the opposite edge of the table. Using that as leverage, he pulled himself, plunging his cock inside her.

"Oh God!" she cried out. Her legs came up to cradle each side of his hips. Grant thrust in and out. Keeping his grip on the edge of the table so he could take her as deep as he possibly could.

"Grant, yes, more," she chanted. And he gave it to her. The table rocked beneath his fucking, and Hannah's perfect body took every inch of him.

She scored her nails down his back, and he hissed. Fucking her harder. Faster.

She tilted her head to the side and bit down on the flexing bicep that was next to her face. That sting of her teeth sinking into his skin, like she was holding on to him in every way she could, made him feel strong. Wild.

"Don't you dare stop. Make me take it," she taunted him. He'd never had a woman like her. A woman who wanted everything he had to give. Could handle it. Begged for more, even.

He bent his head to latch onto her nipple. Sucking hard as he continued to plunge in and out. She cupped his head and held him to her. Her body went still, her muscles tight.

She was close.

And so was he.

But he needed to get her there first. Would die a happy man if he could just feel her come around him.

"Grant . . . ," she whispered. It was the last thing his ears registered, because blood rushed to his face as his release took over. Sinking deep into her, shot after shot of pleasure erupted, and the table creaked under his grip.

That's when he felt it.

Hannah's release.

Her sheath spasmed and sucked him deeper, taking his own orgasm to another level. The feel of her milking him made his body shudder and sensitized his skin. Every inch of her against his body was like a jolt of electricity.

"I love you," he said against her ear. He just didn't know if he said it out loud or only in his lust-wasted mind.

~

Hannah lay in bed, her head on Grant's chest while he played with her hair. They were both staring at the TV across the room, the low hum of the show wafting around them.

"I never would have guessed you liked *Roseanne*," Grant said.

Hannah shrugged against him. "I like the dad in it."

She hadn't meant to say that—it was just the first honest thing that came to mind. She would watch this show when she was young. Back when her father was passed out or busy not noticing her. The dad in the show was funny and had two daughters he clearly cared about. The kind of dad who would hate all boyfriends and fix up an old car for her sixteenth birthday.

Hannah adjusted her position and let out a breath.

"What about your dad?" Grant asked.

"What about him?"

"You haven't said much about him since the grocery store the other day."

She was glad Grant couldn't see her glance away. She didn't know if it was the afterglow of sex or the way Grant was playing with her hair that made her feel warm and safe. But she did one thing she never did . . . she started to talk about her dad.

"He lives around here, and I see him from time to time. Only when he wants something, though."

"What does he want?"

"Money, booze, money for booze." She focused on a freckle on Grant's chest and slowly drew a circle around it with her fingertip. "Or a ride from jail."

Grant's hold on her tightened just enough for Hannah to feel his support.

"Sounds like you've a rough time taking care of him."

"I don't take care of him," she said instantly. "I just try to make sure he doesn't accidentally kill himself or others."

She shook her head against his chest then blew out a breath. "Tell me more about your dad. Or your mom."

Grant let out a small laugh that didn't sound amused at all. "I'll stick with talking about my dad," he said. "He was a romantic. Cared a lot about others. Believed that everyone had a soul mate. Just wish he could have found his."

Hannah glanced up at him. "He didn't find a soul mate in your mom."

"No," Grant said coldly and continued to stare at the TV.

She looked back at his chest, tracing the same freckle. She was getting to know Grant at the same pace as she was letting him get to know her. Parents were a tricky topic for her, and it seemed that Grant could relate. So she'd tread lightly.

"Do you believe in soul mates?" she asked, then instantly hated herself for asking. Because she wasn't sure she wanted to know the answer. At the same time, she really did want to know.

"Yes," he said. "I do."

She bit her bottom lip and wondered what Grant was like as a kid. How his father was with him. He spoke so highly of him that she could almost see a sweet little boy running around his dad's office, lighting up his world.

"He was a hard worker, but he always made time for me," Grant said. Then laughed at the TV. Funny dad struck again, and Grant said, "I can see why you like this show. The dad really is funny."

Hannah snuggled into Grant's chest and settled in for a *Roseanne* marathon. Because between the two of them, the unknown, and the parents that raised them, there was so much unsaid between the sheets they were currently lying in.

And all Hannah could do was try to give a little to get a little, and hope that the pain didn't get too great to handle.

Chapter Nine

A soft mumble was coming from the living room. Hannah frowned, her eyes still closed, her body still sated from the incredible night with Grant. Only Grant wasn't in bed.

She slowly opened her eyes and saw it wasn't even 5:00 a.m. yet.

Her bedroom door was cracked, and she could hear Grant's low voice coming from the living room.

She slowly got up, the cool floor hitting her feet, and she pulled Grant's T-shirt on to ward off the chill in the air. She'd been so warm. So comfortable. She couldn't remember the last time she'd slept so soundly. And she'd been next to Grant.

But this kind of chill went deeper than the air.

"Grant?" she asked, seeing him sitting with his back to her. He turned, his cell phone to his ear, hair still tousled like he'd just gotten out of bed himself.

"Yeah, yeah, we'll discuss this more next week," was all he said into the phone before hanging up.

"Sorry, baby, I didn't mean to wake you," he said, coming to stand before her. His bare chest was warm, and she wanted him nearer. But she couldn't shake the odd scene she'd just walked in on.

"Who was that?" she asked. Then realized it was none of her business, and whatever feeling was taking over her entire chest was heavy and gross.

"The office," he answered simply.

"At five in the morning?"

He smiled. "It's eight a.m. New York time."

That made sense. She just nodded.

"Come on, let's go back to sleep." He ushered her back to bed and got her under the covers. Then climbed in and wrapped her up in his arms.

Hannah lay with her cheek against the heartbeat of the man she'd fallen for six months ago, the man she'd fallen for again today, with the strange notion that she didn't know everything there was to know about Grant Laythem.

~

Yes, Hannah worked at a bar. And yes, she worked the late shift a few nights a week, which meant that yes, she'd deal with drunk people at midnight.

She just wasn't in the mood this particular night.

The place was packed. Everyone was drinking and having a good time. The big fireworks show over the ocean brought in a ton of people. Yachats put on the same show of popping colors lighting up the sky once a month. And after, it seemed like half the town flooded into Goonies. Which was a good thing for the business. But Hannah had a ton on her mind.

Mostly Grant.

"You better watch your mouth," a drunk twenty-something-year-old said to a guy sitting at the bar. Drunk guy was pushy and obviously trying to get close to Hannah to flag her down for another drink. Instead, she walked to the opposite side of the bar and helped the customers there first.

The entire place was loud, and she worked like a robot as various orders got shouted at her.

"Rum and Coke, with a lemon."

"I need a Corona, no lime, and three shots of Cuervo."

"Can I get a sex on the beach and two Coors?"

Hannah made the drinks fast. Popped the tops to the beers and slid them to the customers. Grabbing cash and one credit card to start a tab. She turned to the register, then back to the bar, poured more shots, shook more drinks, more beers . . .

She wondered what Grant was doing. Was he making more mysterious calls? Sure, he'd said it was the office, which made sense, but there was something going on that felt just a little sneaky.

And it was making her brain tick with the slightest anxiety.

Maybe he has another woman in New York?

Tick, tick, tick.

Maybe his business isn't exactly legal?

Tick . . . Tick . . . Tick . . .

Maybe he's hiding something—

"Hey, woman!" the drunk guy yelled and stomped toward her, ramming into people. "I've been waiting on a drink and you're fucking ignoring me!"

"Glad to see you're still astute," Hannah yelled back at him, mixing a martini.

"Bitch," he grumbled, but yeah, she heard it. Every once in a while she got a customer like this. Some douche who got too drunk and mouthed off. She had a bat behind the counter, but in her years of experience, she'd only needed to break it out three times. Which wasn't bad. Occupational hazard.

"Watch it, asshole," Adam, the local mechanic, said to the drunk. The drunk guy shoved Adam, which made the large mechanic stand up, his tattooed muscles pulsing against his T-shirt.

Shit. This was about to get bad.

Adam stepped toward the drunk, and Hannah grabbed her bat and hopped over the bar. Everyone was backing away, creating a small circle of drama and watching intently. The crowd hummed as Hannah got between the two men.

"Adam, go sit down," she said in the cool yet demanding voice she'd come to harness over her almost thirty years. "You, douche bag, get out of my bar."

The drunk laughed at her and then threw his beer glass down, shattering it on the floor.

"No fucking woman is going to tell me what to do," he snarled and took an aggressive step toward her.

Hannah went to hold her bat out, but Adam tugged her back. Hannah wasn't ready for that, and it made her lose her footing. She crashed into a customer, catching an elbow to the eye.

Fuck, that hurts!

She stood just in time to see the drunk take a swing at Adam. The mechanic staggered back, the drunk pressing forward.

"Call the cops," Hannah said to the woman standing near her; she nodded and took out her cell phone. Hannah lunged at the drunk before he could stomp on Adam and hit him in the kneecap, taking him down.

"Fucking bitch!" he yelled.

Then the drunk was off his feet by some magic antigravity breeze... only it wasn't magic at all. It was Grant. He'd come in behind the drunk, lifted him by the shirt, and thrown him back.

Grant's wild dark eyes landed on Hannah, and whatever he saw there infuriated him more. He turned back to the drunk and punched him in the nose, blood gushing instantly.

The drunk wailed in pain and cursed at Grant. "You fucking broke my nose." He couldn't even stand straight, but Grant clearly had no sympathy and threw him out on the street.

The entire bar clapped and cheered, but Grant made a beeline for Hannah, rage and anger and a wild need in his eyes. He grabbed both of her shoulders and shook her.

"What the hell are you doing?" he said loudly.

"I'm breaking up a bar fight," she said, wiggling out of his grip.

"You put yourself between two men twice your size!" He was seething.

"I'm fine. This happens sometimes," she defended.

"Well, I'll be damned if I let it happen again. This is no place for you. You're not staying here."

"Excuse me?" she said. "You have no right to tell me what to do." Grant had never spoken to her like this. Sure, he'd come for her and clearly cared and was protective, but the macho man telling the woman what she could and couldn't do? "What is the matter with you? This is my job, and I can take care of myself."

"Hannah, look at your fucking eye!"

She couldn't. But she could feel it. It was throbbing and hot, and she'd bet she'd have a nice shiner in the morning.

"I wasn't hit—it was part of the scuffle. I caught an elbow."

"Oh, well, then that makes things much better. You still got hurt in a bar fight!"

"Stop yelling at me!" she said. That's when she glanced around and noticed the entire bar watching them. Thank God it was loud, between the music and conversations, but Hannah and Grant were clearly the ones on display.

She took a step toward Grant and lowered her voice. "I get that you're upset with what you saw," she said, "but we'll discuss this later. This is my job, Grant."

"The discussion is over. I've been supportive of your job, but it's not worth you getting physically hurt. That's the line, Hannah. You can't expect me to be okay with you going to work where you could get the shit beat out of you."

She pursed her lips. "It's a bar, Grant. What did you think would happen?"

"I thought it was a sleepy town. Not a place where people brawl. You can't work here. It's unsafe. You're by yourself a lot and you have a damn bat. It's not safe."

Her eyes shot wide. She'd never heard anyone tell her what to do. "You have no right to demand a thing from me."

He shook his head and ran his fingers through his hair. "Of course I don't. Because I'm nothing to you."

She frowned. Where the hell had that come from? Before she could address the look in Grant's eyes, which resembled what she could only guess was fear, red and blue lights flickered outside the bar.

Looked like Gabe had shown up and was dealing with the drunk on the street. At least everyone was looking out the windows and crowding around the door now. This was a sleepy town, and serious brawls didn't really happen. Tonight wasn't that big of a deal. But she couldn't explain that to Grant now.

Grant looked at her and let out a heavy breath. Hannah couldn't shake the feeling that he was exhausted with her. Her stomach burned and bubbled with nerves.

"Come home with me," he said.

She shook her head. "I have to close up. It's last call, and I'll be another half hour."

"Fine," he said and walked past her to sit at the bar. "Last call!" he yelled out to the crowd. It was clear he was going to park his ass right there until Hannah was done and closed and heading home.

With her own heavy exhale, she loosened her grip on the bat and walked behind the bar. She started to pour the last rounds for people and prepared to close. A dark pair of eyes watched her the entire time. How had tonight started with her worrying about Grant and his world and turned into Grant mad at Hannah for her world?

She had a feeling that their worlds were much farther apart than she'd ever thought.

Chapter Ten

Grant was running down the beach for the fourth time in two days. He needed some way to reset his mind. But with every thump of his feet in the sand, he only thought of Hannah more.

It was clear she was giving him the silent treatment lately. He'd felt it the past few days since the "scuffle at the bar," as she'd called it.

He'd call it a brawl that got her hurt. And every time he looked at his beautiful wife and saw the light blue bruise lining her cheekbone near her eye, he wanted to kill that drunk. He didn't give two flying asses that the man hadn't technically hit her. She had gotten hurt. Put herself between two men in a fucking bar fight!

His mind was screaming at him, and Grant just ran faster. With the way he was feeling, he could be halfway to Washington by now. Staying along the beach and pounding sand until he got this rage out of him.

Faster still. Thinking of all the things he wanted to do to Hannah. He wanted to smack her ass and tell her that she was never to put herself in danger. He wanted to toss her over his shoulder and keep her in bed on the brink of orgasm for a week until she was begging and dying from the torture and agreed to any terms he had.

She was stubborn. And she was trying to buy that bar. But he had thought that after that fight, she'd not want a thing to do with the place. Grant had walked in to escort her home and had never been so terrified in his life. Seeing his petite wife get tossed around, then use a bat to defend herself, had made his heart stop.

He'd never seen a woman look so capable yet so fragile in his entire life.

He didn't know what the hell to do. He needed her to come to New York with him now. But she was dead set on owning her bar. Maybe once she got that, she could hire a manager and check in on the place once a month. He'd happily fly here with her to do that. So long as it meant she stayed out of harm's way. He needed to wrap this up, though, because he was done playing. He wanted his wife. Their two weeks had dwindled down to a couple of days and still . . . no sign that she would stay married to him.

He'd made headway, but in the end, he wasn't sure it was enough to convince her to be with him.

Grant was starting to see the familiar beach that was on the back side of Goonies. He was close to home. Decided he should just run there. Hoping Hannah would finally talk to him. Because he was almost out of time, and he'd taken two steps forward with his wife, and then a step back. He needed to get her to agree, once and for all, that they belonged together. Then he could finally get her to come to New York with him, and she could have her bar from afar. What woman wouldn't love that option?

He quickened his pace. Running through town, he rounded the corner and saw Hannah's little place come into view. What he wasn't ready for was the limousine parked in front of it.

He started to slow, breathing hard and putting his hands on his hips as he walked to the limo. The back passenger window rolled down. A tight blonde bun and pair of oversize Dior sunglasses greeted him.

"You know that the closest airport to this godforsaken place is an hour and a half away?" his mother said. Her lips were tight, painted pink, with wrinkles lining them.

"What are you doing here? How did you even find me?" Grant said, furious and yet not completely surprised. His mother opened her car door, forcing Grant to take several steps back. She looked like she always did. Sharp knee-length skirt and matching blazer with dazzling jewelry. She stepped from the car with entitlement and rigid grace.

"Since you've been ignoring my calls, I decided to track you down." She examined her nails. "And I heard there was an investors' meeting this weekend. Thought I'd take the chance to see how you intend to spend my money."

"It's my money, my company. Dad left it to me."

"I'm still his legal widow."

Grant took a deep breath and glanced at the ground. He had to find his calm or he would lose his damn mind.

"You can't contest the will," Grant finally said.

"Oh yes, I can," she said with a happy smile. "And I can even take the company."

Grant laughed. That was the most ridiculous thing he'd ever heard. She could contest the will, fine. Go to trial. Sure. Didn't mean she'd win. Because the will was not only clear about Grant inheriting the estate, but that Grant got the company, and if anything happened to Grant before he could hand it down to his child, it still had to be a Laythem the company went to.

"I don't know how much you're spending on your lawyer, but you can't get the company. And I'm tired of talking to you about this, Mother."

"You treat me worse than your father," she snapped.

"Oh, absolutely I do. Frankly, I'm not sure why he supported you as long as he did, but I won't do the same."

Her grin turned sinister. "Well, it will be interesting to see what the board has to say when they vote in a couple days."

Grant quickly searched his mind. There were no issues to vote on. Nothing on the table.

"Vote?" he asked for clarity.

"Yes. Did you know that the majority of the board at Laythem Incorporated can dictate who is CEO of the company?"

Hot lava fueled only by rage started pumping through his body.

"You cannot get the board to toss me over and elect you CEO." He enunciated every word carefully, because he'd never been so angry in his entire life.

Those lips that he was certain were cemented into a permanent scowl crooked up at the corners with amusement.

"That's up to the board. And you've been playing house, it would seem." She tossed a disapproving look over her shoulder and waved at Hannah's home in dismissal. "Meanwhile, the board is concerned when they don't hear from their CEO in almost two weeks. I'd say that I don't have to toss you over. You're doing a fine job of that on your own, dearest."

She pinched his cheek, and Grant wondered how the woman who'd given him life was so cold. He was nothing to her. He knew that. She cared about money and power. Honestly, he'd always wondered if she'd gotten pregnant with him just to keep her hooks in his father. His father's only mistake in life had been falling for the wrong woman.

"I'm gone for a week and a half and you're threatening a hostile takeover?" he said quietly.

"It's business, dearest. Which is why I'm here," she said with a perk in her voice. "I heard through the grapevine that you're looking to invest in some company around here. A pretty heavy sum."

"So?"

"So, I was curious what has you looking all the way out here and draining the family trust."

He wanted to point out the "family trust" was his father's money and Grant's. Though Grant was new as CEO, he still made good money, contributed to the business, and had been worth millions on his own before his father's will. He didn't owe his mother an explanation about anything. She was sniffing around because she was worried he'd drain the account before she could try to get her talons into it with this contesting-the-will nonsense.

Still, Grant's money was his, and he sure as hell wanted nothing to do with his mother.

He did, however, want his father's company and what he'd left him. Not because he was interested in the extra money or power. It was because he wanted to carry on what his father had built. To add to it. Make him proud. And there was no way in hell he'd let his mother ruin all his father's hard work. She'd sell off the company, bleed it dry, or God knew what. No. He refused to ever let that happen.

"I see your grapevine of spies are still earning their paychecks," Grant said coldly.

"I hardly need spies when three different millionaires come running to one small town. Wasn't exactly detective work, dearest."

Grant took a calming breath, although there was nothing calming about it. His mother had shown up to cause trouble and monitor Grant. Now she knew about the event. He didn't know if she'd go so far as to show up there, but he wanted her gone. At the end of the day, Grant needed her to accept the situation she was in and move on. She had enough money to live on comfortably, but still no technical job, other than a taste for making his life miserable, and Grant had everything to gain.

"I hope you enjoy the Pacific Northwest. Now, if you'll excuse me," he said and started to walk toward the front door when he heard a set of car tires come to a stop in front of the house. He turned and found Hannah getting out of her little car with a bag of groceries in hand.

"Can I help you?" she asked, looking at his mother, who was still in front of her monstrosity of a limo, taking up the entire driveway.

"I highly doubt it, my dear," she said to Hannah.

Hannah frowned, and Grant hustled back to try to head her off.

"Well, this is my driveway you're parked in," Hannah said, walking up.

His mother had that condescending grin again. "Ah, now I see what you've been *doing* out here," she said to Grant, just as he reached by Hannah's side.

He felt rage radiate from Hannah, and Grant couldn't blame her. Hell, he felt it, too. Instead, Hannah turned to Grant and smiled. "Sweetie, if you want to order bitches to be delivered to the house, make sure they come in their original packaging. I think Amazon Prime throws in that option for free now."

Grant wanted to laugh and high-five his wife all at the same time. No one ever spoke to his mother that way, and he liked Hannah's sass coming out. Also nice to know it wasn't reserved for just him.

"Oh, she's a foul-mouthed one." His mother spoke like Hannah wasn't even there, which clearly made the rage boil higher. "Well, take all the time you want in this place. I'll see to things in New York."

She turned and went to get back in her limo.

"You know that'll never happen," Grant said.

"It already is. Have fun with your mistress." She gave another dismissive wave.

Hannah hiked the groceries on one hip, and with more anger and pride than he'd ever heard come from her, she said, "I'm not his mistress, I'm his wife."

That made his mother stop.

Turn.

A look of pure horror washing over her face.

∽

Jesus Christ, what the hell am I doing?

Hannah's brain was churning out a million emotions a million miles a minute. She'd just gone to get groceries, never expecting there to be a fricking limo in her driveway and to be insulted by Joan Rivers's long-lost sister.

And she didn't know what this lady's deal was, but it was clear Grant didn't like her, so she'd felt the need to stand up for him. For herself. For them.

The woman was still by her open-door limo, but for the first time, she looked Hannah in the eye.

"Grant wouldn't be stupid enough to get married," she said.

"I don't know who you think you are, or who you actually are, but you're on my property," Hannah said. "So you can take your overly diamonded-up ass out of here."

The woman smiled wide, and it looked evil. The Botox tried to contain it, but she somehow managed to at least muster a grin.

"Why, my dear, I'm Grant's mother."

Hannah's entire heart dropped to her feet. She had no idea what to say or how to even process that this woman was responsible for Grant's life. She was starting to wonder if this clearly awful woman had something to do with the permanent sadness behind his eyes. The same sadness she knew she had. The kind of sadness that only came from a child of a parent who didn't love them.

And this she wouldn't stand for. Not for Grant. He deserved better. He cared, and this woman—his mother—clearly didn't. She needed to get to the bottom of a few things real quick. Grant had barged into her bar a few days ago and handled things in his way. It was Hannah's turn to step in now.

She handed Grant the bag of groceries. "Please take these inside."

"I'm not leaving you out here with her."

She looked Grant dead in the eye. She needed him to see she could handle herself. She knew they were still not on speaking terms because of the bar fight. But she needed him to believe in her a little bit. She could handle this. She'd been silent in her mind the past few days and trying to figure out what the hell she and Grant were going to do. And if there was any chance of their lives ever merging, she needed to start dealing with the reality of how different their lives were.

She had a drunk slob for a father, and Grant had an evil queen for a mother.

Some fucking fairy tale we're rocking here.

Grant looked at her for a long, long moment. He took the bag and nodded once. There was a flicker in his expression that told her he understood that she needed to be out here, with his mother, for a moment alone.

She watched him go inside and gently shut the front door.

Hannah returned her attention to his mother.

"What is your name, dear?" she asked in a light tone, as if she hadn't just insulted the hell out of Hannah a moment ago.

"Hannah Hastings."

"Well, Miss Hastings. I'm Lillian Laythem. I'm glad to see you didn't take the name, as that would be quite a burden to carry."

"Why are you here?" Hannah asked.

"To see my son. He has his hand in a lot of cookie jars, one of which doesn't belong to him. He's just like his father that way."

"What does that even mean?" Hannah asked, trying for cool, wanting information, but also wanting to slap this woman silly.

"You don't know? Grant's father passed away recently."

"Yes, I do know," Hannah said. She also knew that Grant was still struggling with it. Knew that he didn't talk about his father much without a lot of pain rising up.

"Well, as the widow, I have a vested interest in seeing to my husband's estate. Grant is trying to take everything from me."

"Grant wouldn't do that."

"Oh? Because you know him so well? His father was a romantic, too. Fell head over heels for me. Then he grew tired of me and was on to the next woman, the next adventure. And yet, I looked the other way. Stayed his devoted wife while he lived an entirely different life without me." She paused for a dramatic sigh. "I hope you were wise enough to sign a prenup, because when this fight over my dearly beloved's estate is settled, Grant is going to come out in the hole. If he doesn't drag you down with him first."

She turned to get into her car. "You may want to think about what I'm telling you, dear. The Laythem men are takers. They take your youth, your heart, your money, and try to leave you with nothing."

She closed the door, and Hannah stood there, having no idea why bile was rising in her throat and she felt the need to retch.

As she watched the limo back out of her driveway and pull away, she wondered how much of what Lillian had just said was applicable to Hannah. Grant had already threatened to take her bar if she hadn't given him the two weeks of trying to make it work. Was he really just an adrenaline chaser? Only wanting her because she was a challenge?

No . . . she didn't think so. She thought back to the way he held her, the way he fought for her, the way he owned her . . .

But she liked that. Asked for that.

She shook her head. She didn't know what to think. She did know that people weren't always what they seemed. She just needed to know if it was Grant or Lillian who had the false front.

She walked inside and found Grant with his palms on the edge of the table, leaning over it. He was sweaty from what looked like a run, his T-shirt clinging to his muscles, and black shorts showing off his tan, toned calves.

"Hannah, are you okay?" he said, walking toward her.

He hugged her and then set her away to look her in the eyes.

"I'm fine. What, did you think she'd hit me or something?"

"No, she has a way of spinning lies to make people feel like shit."

She looked at Grant. At her husband. The man she'd said yes to after two weeks, and she wondered how she'd got in this mess. How she felt like she knew him so well, yet maybe didn't.

No, she did. She had to. Because if there was one thing she trusted, it was her gut. And deep down she knew Grant was a good man. He wouldn't lie to her, take everything from her. He wouldn't.

"She talked about your dad," Hannah started slowly. Grant's face twisted from anger to sadness, back to anger. It was clear how much he loved his father and how much pain he was still in from the loss. There had been no sign of any emotion other than bitchiness on Lillian's face.

"I don't need to know what she said to you about him." Grant's dark eyes stared straight through her own and into her soul. "The only thing that is important to me is that you know he was a good man. The only mistake he ever made was loving her. She took everything from him. Even now, she's still trying to take everything."

Hannah frowned. Lillian had said exactly the opposite. But she had also said that while being frosted in diamonds like a frickin' blonde Elizabeth Taylor. Hannah was more and more confident that she knew Grant, and if his mother was a sign of anything, it was what Grant had had to struggle with his whole life. Hannah would never want anyone, especially him, to judge her based on her father. So she wouldn't do that to him. She'd believe him.

Trust in him.

"I have no doubt your father was a wonderful man."

Grant nodded once. "Thank you. Did she say anything else? Why she was here?"

"She said she was here to see you. You're trying to take what's hers? Something like that."

Grant breathed deep. "I'm not taking anything from her."

"I believe you," Hannah said. And she did. She honestly did. She'd suspected that Grant was well off, and now seeing his mom, that was confirmed. But what she didn't know were the details. Would he really be in the hole? The term *prenup* stuck in her mind, and she couldn't figure out why it refused to unstick. *Only one way to get a gauge on this . . .*

"She asked if we'd signed a prenup."

Grant's eyes darkened, and his expression shifted just enough that she could tell he didn't like that.

"We don't need one," he said shortly.

Hanna's chest stalled. "How come?"

He cupped her face. "Because I trust you." He searched her face. "Do you trust me?"

She looked at him. Those deep pools pulling her in. His warm hands, capable yet gentle on her face.

"Yes, I do trust you," she whispered.

He kissed her softly. "I'm sorry about the other night at the bar."

She nodded. "I'm sorry, too."

"I just can't lose you. The thought of anything happening to you . . ."

"I'm okay," she said. "This is my life here. You have to trust me that I can handle things."

"I want you happy. I know you love that bar. I still hate you having to throw yourself into something dangerous."

She nodded. "I know. And I hate that I feel like I don't quite know everything there is to know about you."

The tip of his nose brushed hers, but he didn't say anything. He just hugged her close, and Hannah let his warmth wrap around her. Her heart recognizing him, needing him. Her mind ticking once more . . .

Maybe we really are too different to ever work.

Chapter Eleven

Hannah sat at the little desk in Laura's flower shop. The front part of Baughman Home Goods was Laura's display of various flowers and arrangements. It was small and cute and all her style. The back warehouse was where Jake worked.

"These arrangements are looking great," Hannah said. Laura was putting several centerpieces together for the event tomorrow night. Looked like the hiring company had gone local for not just the bar—which was Hannah's job—but the flowers and food, too. Laura's flowers would be on display at the event, and she was proud of her friend for all the hard work she'd put into making her business a success.

"Thank you! I'm so excited for this job. I love getting to put arrangements together. I haven't done it much lately, since I've been doing more landscaping stuff."

"Well, they look wonderful," Hannah said, handing her another flower. "How do you and Jake do it? You two are different, yet you work together and live together."

"Great sex," Laura said with a smile, adding a rose to the arrangement.

Hannah raised a brow. "I guess that counts for something." She snipped another flower and handed it to Laura.

"I mean, nothing is ever easy, including our relationship. It took a lot of hard work, and yes, we're different. Remember what we went through when I first came back to town?"

"You two fought and hated each other," Hannah recalled.

"Which, again, made for great sex, but we had to meet each other halfway."

"I don't know how to do that without knowing everything will work out."

Laura laughed. "You don't know everything will work out. Because there's no way to know. You just have to have faith it will. Go into it knowing that you're going to try your damnedest and you love him. That's what you know."

"Yeah . . . ," Hannah said quietly. Then frowned. "Wait, what makes you think I love Grant?"

Laura grabbed a lily, put it in the arrangement, and spun the vase. "Because I can see it. You're trying so hard not to count on him. You're actually trying not to love him. But you do. You have. Which is why you married him on a damn boat."

Laura shot her a playful smile.

There was that. Hannah had never been impulsive like that. She knew then and still did now that Grant was special. She thought back to what Grant had said to her that night at dinner . . .

You love me. Stop acting like you don't . . .

Was that what she was doing? Trying to find any reason to remind herself why this was a bad idea? Why Grant was a bad idea. Because he was the only one that could hurt her. Which meant that . . .

Crap. I really love him.

"You can't control everything," Laura said, keeping her eyes on her vase.

It hit Hannah just then, the connection she and Grant had. She tried to deal with so much, tried to be in control and plan for the worst. Deal with endless responsibilities. But Grant took care of her. Let her be free. He took over, and she felt truly seen and taken care of.

"I trust him more than I even knew," she said.

"Duh," Laura said, grabbing a carnation out of Hannah's hand.

"But that doesn't mean we're right for each other. Or can even make this work," Hannah said.

Laura stopped fussing with her flowers and stared at Hannah.

"Right for each other?" she repeated in a snippy tone. "You're the most stubborn, pain-in-the-butt person I've ever known. And you finally met your match. You're not right for each other—you're perfect."

Hannah glanced down. She wondered what it was about her that made Grant want her. He challenged her, and she challenged him back. There was a lot of push and pull and . . . spankings.

But she really did feel herself with him. Felt like he saw her for her. Never a local, never trash, never mean . . . he embraced her difficult side and matched it.

"Of all the times a man has never shown up for you," Laura said, "Grant has. Even after you ran. And Jake did the same thing for me."

Hannah thought hard about what her friend was saying. And she was right. There was something special between her and Grant, and it deserved a chance. A real chance for her to trust in what they could be. Her gut had told her once before that he was it. Now it was time to listen to it again.

Maybe Grant would stay here. Maybe at the end of these two weeks, she'd be his wife, just like he wanted. Then they could really try to make this work. There was no way to know unless they tried. And damn the man, but he might have just gotten her to fall in love with him again.

"I think I need to go to work. Then I'll find Grant for a little chat."

"I think you should. Maybe say something nice," Laura offered.

"I was going to start with, 'Hey, jackass, congratulations—you wore me down. Wanna bone?'"

Laura rolled her eyes. "Well, that's one of the most romantic things I've ever heard you say."

Hannah waved to her friend and headed out. She needed to find the only nonlocal in town and admit she might want to give their marriage a shot after all.

"What do you mean, you can't get here? You're my lawyer, Harvey, and I have a big investing deal that is set to close tomorrow night."

"Grant," Harvey said from the other end of Grant's cell phone, "you need to get to New York. Your mother is taking you to trial over contesting the will, and the board is meeting tomorrow to vote on you. She's wreaking havoc here."

"Then why the hell did she come here for a day?" Grant said, but his mind instantly churned out the answer. She was checking up on him. Seeing if he was up to something. Spreading misery. She never wanted to go to the investment event. She'd come out for just a day to make his life miserable.

"She'll be around for that meeting tomorrow?" Grant asked.

"Yes," Harvey said. "Her lawyer has been calling me all day. She lands today. She's bringing the full-court press."

"She doesn't have a case."

"No, but she can still try to take over your spot as CEO, which will give her power and access to Laythem holdings. Grant, I'm telling you, as your attorney, you need to get back here."

He closed his eyes for a moment and knew Harvey was right. If he wanted to save his father's company, he needed to get to New York and talk to his board.

Grant paced in the living room. The event was tomorrow. But so was the board meeting.

"I'll be on the next flight to New York."

He hung his phone up and threw it, cursing his mother, God, and every other thing in the world that was keeping him from the woman he loved.

A woman that he wasn't sure would ever give their marriage a chance. And he had to save something . . . at least he'd save his father's company, if nothing else. Even if the cost was blowing a chance with the only woman he'd ever loved, who might never love him back.

But he had to be sure.

Had to hear it from her.

His father had died telling Grant that the most important thing in life was finding genuine happiness with a genuine person you could spend your life with. His father had never had that. He'd had his heart ripped out by a gold digger, and Grant had been around the social scene in New York enough to know that Hannah was the only woman he'd ever met with real warmth to her.

He loved her.

But he couldn't make her love him, want him, or their marriage. Despite his best efforts.

"I still have to hear it from her," he said to himself as he grabbed his jacket and headed out the front door. He walked quickly down the side street that came out to hit Main. Several blocks down, he finally made it to Goonies.

The afternoon sun was bright but not warm. His chest hurt from the cool air, or maybe it was his nerves. Knowing he was walking into one of the biggest conversations of his life.

He opened the bar door and saw Hannah.

She was behind the bar, wearing a black tank top, her hair in a long braid, making her creamy skin sparkle. He watched her tuck a lock of hair that came loose behind her ear, then wipe the counter down.

She was beautiful.

He wanted to watch her, remember this moment. Because right then, Hannah was his wife, and she was happy.

He walked toward her.

"Hey," she said with a smile. "What can I get you, Mr. Laythem?"

He placed his hands on the bar. "An answer," he said.

She frowned, then glanced around. He walked to the end of the bar, where they could have a little privacy.

"What are you talking about?" she asked in a hushed tone.

"Us, Hannah. I need to know. Are you going to stay married to me?"

"Why are you asking me this? I thought you had two weeks and—"

"I need to know now." He would never walk out on her, but he couldn't let his father's business crumble. He couldn't fail at one for the other, especially if the other didn't want him back.

"Why is there a time crunch all of a sudden?" she asked.

"There's always been a time crunch," he said. He didn't know why she looked so concerned. Maybe that was his answer. That despite everything, she would still go her separate way from him. He'd never told her how much money he had or the details of his mother and her crazy lies and schemes to take the company. Hannah knew enough. And he wanted her to make her choice based on him. Not anything else.

"Is this about what's going on with your mom? Do you need help? Are you . . . struggling?"

He frowned. Did he need help? What the hell was she talking about?

"I need my wife, Hannah," he said. "I need to know if you're in this with me for good. If you'll give us a chance."

"What's going on, Grant? I know you don't tell me everything and have secret calls and all that, but this feels like a setup for failure."

Her words hit his chest like a spear. "Setup for failure," he repeated.

She leaned over and kept eye contact. "Grant, what is going on? You're being cryptic, and I can't commit to something when I don't know enough about what you're asking me to sign up for."

"You married me already. So you already signed up. I want to know if you're still in it."

Her lips parted, and Grant felt his stomach churn with fear. He needed her to have faith in him, in them, and the way her gaze searched his face, he didn't think she did.

She didn't answer. Looked confused and scared and sad.

His wife looked sad.

"Will you come to New York with me?" he asked. Trying a simpler route.

"I can't leave work. I'm trying to buy this place, and the deal closes soon."

"I'll make sure you can travel to look over the bar several times a year," he offered. "I'll make sure the deal closes fine. Come to New York with me."

"What? Are you asking me to move to New York and leave my entire life here behind?"

"What did you think this was, Hannah?"

"I thought this was us seeing if we had a shot. You are the one who started this whole thing."

"You are the one that left me in the first place."

Anger was rising. He tried to retrace his words to figure out how this had gone from seeing his wife happy to fighting in a bar and his heart being slowly suffocated like a heavy boot was pressing down on it.

"I can't move to New York, Grant."

He stared at her lovely face. Watched that single lock of hair slip off her ear and brush her face. He wanted to reach out and run his fingers through it.

She glanced down at her hands and lightly chewed on her bottom lip. "Why don't you stay here?" she said softly.

Grant frowned. "There's no way I can stay here, Hannah. I have a company and responsibilities in New York. I can't live in Yachats."

She faced him fully, something like hurt and anger washing over her face. "Why the hell did you come here, then? Why were you pushing for us to work if you can't live here?" Then her eyes went wide. "You assumed I'd leave my Podunk small-town life and just follow you."

The realization sounded blunt when she said it like that. But yes, that was what he'd thought.

"I'm offering you the best of both worlds. You can visit Yachats. Have your bar."

"You can visit New York, have your company."

He shook his head. "It's not that simple."

"No shit, Grant!" she snapped.

He took a step back. "We won't work . . . will we?" he asked.

"I can't move to New York," she answered.

That was the answer he was afraid of. He couldn't have both. Couldn't save his father's company and his legacy and have Hannah. The empty space in his chest where Hannah had put warmth started to pulse cold. He was four feet away from her, and already, he felt the thousands of miles closing in.

"Understood," he said.

He looked at her. Watched her perfect face contort with confusion, pain, and if he looked hard enough, he could see love there.

Too bad he knew better than to think he'd seen that.

He turned and walked out of the bar, the smallest sound of Hannah calling his name echoing in his ears as he let the door shut behind him.

∼

It was the last day of the cruise. The sunrise as the boat docked in Cozumel was the second-best sight Grant had ever seen. The first was the woman he'd fallen in love with on this boat over the past two weeks.

Hannah slept with her head on his chest, her black hair splayed out over him. He ran his fingers through it as he looked out the deck window from the bed in his stateroom.

Sunrise.

A new day.

The last day.

He had twenty-four hours left with this woman. Come this time tomorrow, they'd be docking in the States and going back to reality. Their separate ways. A fact Grant couldn't bear to think about.

She stretched and smiled, and he kissed the top of her head.

"What are we going to do today?" she asked in a sleepy voice. And Grant knew the only thing he wanted to do was to make her his. Forever.

"Something special," he promised.

∾

The little van that Grant had rented bumped along the dirt road all around Cozumel. After getting out of the city and dock area, Grant had arranged for a tour guide to take them around the water's edge.

The driver said something to Grant in Spanish and pulled over to the side of the road. Hannah looked out and saw the lovely, lush green jungle on one side of the road and the bright blue ocean on the other side.

Grant got out of the van and helped her down.

"Where are we going?" she asked.

"Exploring," he said and took her hand and guided her toward the water.

The road and cliff gave way to finely grained sand as they walked toward the Caribbean Sea. Grant clutched her hand tighter as they dipped their toes in.

"This is the most incredible sight I've ever seen," she breathed. The clear blue water was endless. A kind of color she only saw in magazines. And she was standing there, in the middle of the sunshine, and felt grateful. Grateful to have Grant to share this with.

She closed her eyes and could smell his spicy scent drift over the sea air. Feel his warm hand in hers. Allow the waves to tickle her toes.

She felt one with him.

With the earth.

Complete.

"I love you," she said, smiling, and felt every word. From her feet to her ears, she loved Grant.

She opened her eyes and turned to look at him, but he wasn't eye to eye with her.

He was kneeling.

The small crash of waves hit his ankle and thigh as he knelt there on a single knee.

"Hannah." He looked up at her and gripped her hand in both of his. "Don't let this end."

She frowned down at him. "What?" she whispered.

"Don't let this end between us."

"I don't understand what you're asking of me," she said.

His eyes were dark and bright. "I'm asking you to be mine forever. Marry me, Hannah. Because I don't want to go back to a life without you."

Her lips parted, and she couldn't see anything past the face of the man before her. On a knee, wanting her forever.

No one ever stuck around for her.

"Grant . . . ," she whispered. "I don't want to go back to a life without you, either."

A wide smile split his face. "Is that a yes, Miss Hastings?"

She nodded. "Yes."

He rose and cupped her face in both hands, kissing every breath out of her until all she could breathe in was him.

"I'm never letting you go now," he said against her mouth. And for the first time ever, Hannah believed in a man's words.

Chapter Twelve

Hannah walked through the front door of her home. She'd been practicing what to say to Grant since he'd left earlier. All day she'd thought of him. Of what the hell was going on. She didn't have details and hated that his awful mother's voice spun through her head.

Why was he in this sudden time crunch? He'd bounded into the bar looking crazed and lost and sad. Was something happening in his company? Was he losing everything, like his mother had said? He wanted Hannah to jump blindly, and she had no idea what to think.

Her heart was in pieces, because he had assumed she'd just follow him. Yet he wouldn't entertain the idea of moving here. She'd worked her butt off for years, finally was closing in on owning the bar, and had an important event tomorrow that would allow her to do so.

And he dismissed it like it was some hobby.

But she loved him . . .

She needed to talk to him. To figure things out once and for all without feeling like she'd been ambushed at work. There was hope still . . . right?

She walked through the door, but the house was empty. It felt colder, too. Like his entire presence was gone.

The only thing that lingered was his memory. From the couch, to the kitchen table, she saw him among her things. In her home. Yet he was gone.

She found a note on the kitchen counter.

Hannah,
I had to fly back to New York. I wish it had been with you. But maybe you're right . . . our lives are too different. Thank you for being my wife while it lasted. You should have everything you want in life. I'll be in touch with details about dissolving our union.

Love, Grant

The note slipped from Hannah's fingers, and an instant pain erupted in her chest. Like someone had lit fire to her ribs, and they were charring and burning like old driftwood. She couldn't breathe. Her knees wobbled, her calves turning to mush instead of muscle.

"'Love, Grant'?" she repeated out loud. *"Love?"*

She didn't feel loved. She felt betrayed. Shortchanged. She'd really thought they still had two days. Sure, she had Cal's event to bartend at tomorrow, but they still had two days. But he was gone.

He'd left her.

The Laythem men are takers. They take your youth, your heart, your money, and try to leave you with nothing . . .

All Hannah cared about was her heart. Because for the first time, she truly felt what it was like to be cast off. She'd come to want Grant. Need him. Trust him.

Should have known better.

She looked around, and her skin itched with the need to leave. She couldn't be in her own home because he was so real to her there. She needed to get away. So she went to the only place she could to outrun the loneliness. She went back to Goonies.

"Weren't you just here?" Rudy teased, keeping court with only three customers. Thankfully it was a slow day.

"Yeah, I just needed to get out of my house," she said honestly and walked up to the bar.

"You still good to go to buy this place?" Rudy said.

Hannah nodded, and he slid her a beer. "I get my big check from this event in the mail today. Then we're good to go," Hannah said.

"Excellent. I get out of this place, and you get in it. Dreams do come true."

Hannah clinked her longneck with his and took a sip. She needed to focus on something other than Grant and the gaping hole growing deeper in her ribs.

"Hey, Hannah," Cal said, coming to sit beside her at the bar.

"Hey, what are you doing here?" she asked.

"Ah, just taking a break from working. Long hours this week. But I'm excited for tomorrow night."

Hannah frowned. "You're going to be at the event?"

"Yeah, it's kind of my deal. Well, Grant put it on. Investors are coming to the subdivision to see my buildings, and they're talking about kicking in as backers to get my business expanding."

Hannah had been hit with too much information at once.

"Wait, Grant put this on? This event?" Hannah searched her mind—the woman she'd been working with was named Sarah. What the hell did Grant want with investing here?

"Yeah, he's thinking of investing and brought a few guys form New York out. Though he said he had an emergency, so he won't make it. But he already cut me a check and went all in. I have my first project funded by him already. The other investors are still coming, too, so that's even more opportunity."

"Whoa." Hannah faced Cal fully, trying to piece all of this together. So Grant got hold of Cal to let him know he wasn't coming to an event he'd planned? And he'd invested money into Cal's business.

Which meant . . .

"Grant is hosting the event, so he hired all the people to put it on," she muttered. And he had more money than she'd thought. Not that it mattered, but it was starting to make sense why his mother was fighting for it.

She has a way of spinning lies to make people feel like shit . . .

"Yeah, that would make sense," Cal said.

"And he's an investor?" Hannah asked.

Cal frowned. "He was specific on keeping his involvement on the down low."

"That bastard told you not to tell me what he did?" That was the secret. The reason she felt out of the loop.

Cal shrugged. "I did some research, and I can understand why. The guy is worth millions. Like, a ton of millions."

Cal pulled up his phone and showed Hannah an article on Grant Laythem and Laythem Inc. He was a huge deal in New York and had a ton of money and . . .

"He lied to me," she breathed. But not in the way she'd thought. She'd thought he was in trouble. Trying to nail her down and use her. When, really, he was the one with a ton of money and working behind the scenes.

Yes, she'd known Grant had some kind of money. But not like this. She'd had no idea he was stupidly wealthy.

"Hey, Hannah," Rudy called from behind the bar and hung up the phone. "That was the bank. The loan has been paid and a bid put in on this bar."

"What?" Hannah all but screamed.

"I don't know what that means . . . did someone just buy this place out from under you?" Rudy asked her, as if she had a clue herself.

Hannah's eyes went wide, and she looked at Cal. "What's the first project Grant hired you for?"

Cal glanced down. "Remodeling this bar."

Hannah's entire chest caved in on itself. Grant had taken everything. Her love, her dreams, her bar . . . and he'd left.

She couldn't focus or fathom what was happening—all she could do was try not to cry as she felt her heart shatter into a million pieces and cut her up from the inside out.

Chapter Thirteen

A loud knock on the door made Hannah frown deep in her sleep. Her head was pounding. Her mouth was dry.

Shit, I'm hungover.

The knock sounded again, and she peeked open one eye to see she was on her couch in the living room, fully clothed, and it was sunny outside.

She let out a loud breath and slowly got up. She had the event tonight, which meant she had several hours until then to think about all the shit that had rained down in the past twenty-four hours. Apparently five drinks at Goonies didn't numb the pain of Grant lying to her, leaving her, then stealing her bar out from under her.

The knocking sounded again, and she realized it was coming from the front door. She got up and ambled to the entrance. She opened the door to find the last person she'd ever expected to see.

"Silas?" she asked her father, who was standing on her front stoop looking surprisingly awake.

"I just stopped by to see how you were feeling," he said. There was no slur in his voice. No staggering stance or smell of fresh gin on his breath. He didn't look great, but he didn't look drunk. So that was a start.

"I'm fine," she lied.

Her father looked her over, and Hannah shielded a hand over her eyebrows to try to shut out the bright sunlight.

"You look like shit," he said.

"Well, thanks for never sugarcoating. Anything else you want to say?" she replied with annoyance.

"Yeah, there is," he said. "Stop being a dumbass."

She closed her eyes for a moment and rested her shoulder against the doorjamb. "If I wanted you to come over and insult me, I would have called."

"This isn't an insult—this is free advice."

"Oh, really? What a gem coming from you."

"Hey, I know what I'm talking about, you brat. I'm here to tell you to stop."

She laughed. "Stop what? What are you even talking about?"

"I'm talking about you. Last night at Goonies."

She pinched her nose. He must have seen her. "Jesus, Silas. Just because I have a few drinks one night doesn't mean I want a wake-up call of you in my face."

"It wasn't a few drinks. I knew what you were doing."

"And what's that?" she said, exasperated.

"You were drowning your sorrows in liquor. You wanna drink, fine. But don't you go hiding behind the bottle. You're better than that."

Those last words made Hannah's heart snap into motion. It was the only kind thing she could remember her father saying to her. And he sounded like he actually meant it. Still, she didn't need him all of a sudden. And she certainly didn't need his advice.

"You see me in a bar once, and now you think you know who I am?" she said to him.

"Yes, I know who you are. You don't go giving in to your grief and unleashing your anger on yourself through drink. But that's what you did last night."

"How on earth do you think you have this much insight?"

"Because," he snapped, "I've been doing the same thing for over twenty years." Her father sighed and ran a hand through his greasy hair. "I broke when your mama left us. Hated life. Hated you, even, a little. A constant reminder that she's gone."

While parts of that hurt, he was trying to be honest, so she kept quiet and let him finish.

"You're better than me, Hannah. You always have been. You're tough, and whatever you're going through, don't you let it take you down."

He nodded once, lifted his hand like he was going to wave, then set it down as if he thought better of it.

"That's all I came to say," he muttered, then turned to leave.

"Dad?" she asked, and he turned to face her. "You came to check on me?"

He nodded. "You looked like you were in pain last night. Wanted to make sure you got home all right."

He walked down her driveway and to the street. A sting hit hard behind her eyes, and she had to close them to alleviate the burn. Her father, whom she'd bailed out over and over, had actually come to check on her.

She didn't remember seeing him last night. Didn't remember much other than with every drink, she'd felt a little more numb. Because the hurt of losing Grant, of the secrets, was too much to bear.

She watched her father walk away and realize that he thought she was strong. In his way, he cared. And it was up to Hannah not to let these issues take her down. Her dreams were still her own. She'd fight for her bar, for her future.

She'd get to the bottom of whatever the hell Grant had been thinking.

She went back into her house, closed the front door, and picked up her cell phone. She dialed Becky Lace at the local bank. They'd gone to school together and had gotten along pretty well. Now, as adults, Becky had been working with Hannah to get the loan for the bar, and every time Becky came into Goonies, she drank for free. It was the silent understanding they had.

"Yachats Bank, this is Becky, how can I help you?"

"Hey, Becky, it's Hannah Hastings."

"Oh, hi," she said joyfully.

"I know this is unconventional, but I need to know what's going on with the bar. Rudy said someone put an offer on it. It's not even on the market."

"Yes, well, the person must have known it was up for sale," she said with tone of a professional courtesy.

"So I can't buy it now? I have the money. I'm paying the balloon payment tomorrow."

"That's been paid off, and the bar has actually been sold as of this morning. Rudy signed off on the sale and paperwork."

Rudy? So he'd gone with another buyer? Even after he made a deal with Hannah? She was ready to burst with frustration.

"Who did Rudy sell it to?" Hannah asked slowly.

She could hear Becky's frown from the other side of the line. "He sold it to you," she said.

Hannah about swallowed her tongue. "What are you talking about?"

"The bar was sold, cash up front, and put in your name," Becky said.

Hannah's mouth hung open, and before she could ask more, her other line beeped.

"Hey, Becky, let me call you back." She switched over to the other line and answered the number she didn't recognize. "Hello?"

"Hello. I'm looking for Hannah Hastings?" a man asked.

"This is she," she replied.

"Miss Hastings, I'm Harvey Wolcott, Mr. Laythem's attorney. I need to discuss some legal matters with you."

She closed her eyes. This was the call she'd been waiting for. The one that ended any tie she had with Grant. And her heart sank.

"Okay," she urged.

"Miss Hastings, you have been awarded an eighty percent share in Laythem Inc., as well as sole proprietorship of Mr. Grant Laythem the Third's estate in its entirety."

"What in the hell are you talking about?" she said around a strangled breath. Had the world gone mad today? "Grant Laythem left and . . ."

"And you're his legal wife. He has bestowed his entire estate on you."

She gripped her head and tried to wrap her hungover mind around what was going on.

So Grant hadn't left her with nothing—he'd left her with *everything*. But he'd still left . . .

"Miss Hastings?" Harvey asked from the other line.

"Yes, I'm here," she said.

"I was hoping to set up a time I can get you some documents."

"Sure. Are you calling from New York?"

"Yes, ma'am."

She thought of Harvey, of Grant, sitting around in a big high-rise in the middle of downtown Manhattan. At least, that's what it looked like from the picture Cal had shown her last night of where Laythem Inc. was located.

"Do you mind if I call you back? I need to get a few details sorted out," she said to Harvey.

"Of course. Thank you, Miss Hastings."

She looked at her phone and hung up. Wishing Grant was in front of her so she could hug him—or scream at him.

Chapter Fourteen

Grant sat at the large rectangular table in the Laythem Inc. conference room. He sat back in his chair, his three-piece suit feeling a little constrictive. He glanced out at the view of Manhattan from the wraparound windows on the fiftieth floor.

He wasn't in Yachats anymore.

And yet, he should feel comfortable. He should feel at home. But he didn't. He thought of Hannah. Glanced at his watch and knew she was getting ready for the event. Knew she hated him by now. Or maybe she didn't care. Either way, it wouldn't be long before she realized what Grant had done regarding the bar. He'd meant it when he'd said she should have everything she wanted in life. Even if it broke his chest in half that he wasn't one of them.

She might not want him, but he trusted her. So much that he'd stake everything he had on it. Risk everything.

Then why the fuck are you sitting here instead of being with Hannah?

He glanced at the twelve board members around the table. He had come back for this. Walked out on her, to sit here with a dozen old men waiting to vote on who got to run this company. All he wanted was be back with Hannah. In her little house. Maybe working with Cal on his business. Opening his own investing firm on that little Main Street.

All of those ideas were ridiculous. Because Hannah didn't want him.

His father always told him that a good businessman knew when to cut his losses. Too bad Grant's entire stomach was aching at the fact that he'd left his wife. They were over. And they'd never had a chance. She was right. Whatever they saw in each other had been impulsive.

So why did he want to get the hell out of there and find the next plane to Oregon?

"Let it be noted in the minutes that Laythem Inc. is set to vote on a proposal for a change in CEO," seventy-year-old, white-haired Gary said.

Grant sat forward in his chair. He was a member of his own damn board, which meant he had a say, and thank God his mother wasn't there. Though she was likely lurking somewhere around the skyscraper waiting for word on if she was going to inherit a huge company.

"Shall we take a vote on the matter of Grant Laythem remaining CEO of Laythem Inc.?" Gary initiated and looked around at everyone ready to cast their hand for or against Grant in keeping his father's company.

∽

Grant finally exited the conference room, rubbing his temples between his thumb and middle finger.

"Grant?" Harvey called, hustling up to him. "We need to talk. There's a situation."

"Seriously, Harvey, I can't right now. I've been in that damn meeting for over three hours, I'm hungry, and I need a minute to process everything." Grant picked up his pace, hoping Harvey would get the hint, and headed to his office down the hall. He was reeling from the stress of the last few hours and hadn't realized he'd literally sat on the edge of his seat for damn near the entire thing.

"But, Grant, there's—"

"Seriously, Harvey, I can't take on more drama until I decompress." As soon as the words left his mouth, he rounded the corner to his office and heard someone yelling.

"I don't give a good goddamn if he's in a meeting. I said I'd wait. And I'm waiting."

He recognized that voice. That vicious, sexy, stubborn voice.

He walked into his office sitting area to see poor Sarah, his assistant, trying to kick Hannah out.

"Hannah," Grant breathed, taking in the sight of her. She was in ripped jeans and a T-shirt, and her hair was messy, like she'd been on a plane for five hours. Which clearly she had been, since she was standing in front of him.

Her blue eyes turned to lasers. "You," she said and stomped toward him. "You have no right to give me all of your shit. I was just telling Harvey that and he ran off—" She glared at Harvey, who was now hiding behind Grant.

Grant chuckled. God, he'd missed her and her sass. The woman could take care of herself. He had no doubt. But she also made everyone pay for undermining her. He had to be careful how he played this, though. She was here, in New York, to see him. He couldn't falter or give in. He had to feel her out. It had broken his heart once when she'd told him no—he couldn't bear to hear it again. So he had to stay calm, cool, and collected.

"Why don't we take this in my office?" Grant said and showed her to the adjoining door. "Sarah, hold my calls."

He walked her into his office and unbuttoned his jacket as he sat behind his desk and grabbed a bottle of Jack and two tumblers from the bottom drawer.

He poured the liquor and slid her a glass. She just walked up to the desk, placed her hands on it, and leaned toward him.

"What the hell are you doing?" she asked him harshly.

"I was going to ask you the same thing," he said, taking a sip of his drink. Playing the part of calm and cool was tough, since her mouth looked so damn kissable.

Focus, Grant.

"I'm here because six months ago you rode in on a boat to fuck with my life, then two weeks ago you rode in on a plane to fuck with my life. Now I'm just waiting for you to book a train ticket and really round out your mission of messing with me through all modes of transportation."

He grinned. "Well, I'm very well versed in travel methods."

"Don't play cocky business mogul with me. You have single-handedly put your mark on everything I care about."

He frowned. "Speaking of what you care about"—snark came out, because he was hurt she was talking about her bar rather than him—"why aren't you serving drinks at Cal's event tonight? I thought that was an important job to you."

"It was, until I found out you set it up. And you already bought the bar."

"It's not my bar," he said quietly.

"I never asked you to come in and fix my life. I was doing fine. I can take care of myself. I could have bought the bar myself."

"Yes, I'm aware. You can do everything by yourself, Hannah."

She straightened and kept her eyes on him, but there was a softness now.

"I never would have taken anything from you. I tried to give you everything. I hired Cal to remodel Goonies however you want. It's yours."

She shook her head. "That's not what I wanted."

"Bullshit," he said, his calm getting tougher to cling to. "All you talked about was that bar. Your home. You picked it over me. Over us. I wanted you to have it. I understand."

"No, you idiot, I wanted you!" she said.

Grant frowned.

"You just didn't give me a chance. You kept secrets. Worked behind my back instead of with me. Why? Why wouldn't you just tell me you're a bazillionaire and had all these deals you were setting up in my town? Why go behind my back? I trusted you, and you kept secrets."

"Because I wanted you to want me for me," he said. "I didn't want money to get in the way." He'd grown up with a woman who valued money over her son. Only had unsuccessful relationships with women who wanted his money more than him. He wanted Hannah to be different. She was different. And part of him hadn't realized how scared he'd been of that.

She shook her head. "I could give a shit about money. I care about the man you are. You should have told me."

She blew out a breath, picked up her glass, downed the drink in one swallow, and placed it back on his desk.

"I wanted you, not all your shit."

"Charming sentiment, baby."

"Well, whatever. I don't know why you put all your 'estate'"—she air quoted the last word, and Grant figured Harvey had called her about what he'd set into motion—"in my name, but I don't want it."

"I put it in your name because I trust you. Because you're a Laythem. Because my mother was coming after my father's assets, the company, all of it. So I had to transfer everything to a safe place with a person I trusted."

She took a few steps around the room, then back. Pacing. Then she scoffed. "Here I thought you were trying to take things from me, when in reality, you gave everything you had to me. You have way more to lose on paper."

Grant nodded.

But her eyes were bright and blue and sad when they met his. "But off paper, I lost big. Because you took my heart and soul when you walked out."

Grant watched water fill her eyes, and it was like a punch to the gut. He never wanted to make Hannah cry. Ever. And she stood there, totally right.

He'd gone about everything backward. Let himself get caught up in things that didn't matter. Let himself get caught up in his own secrets and fears. He should have trusted her to handle it. All of it.

She walked to his office door, then turned to face him. "I came here to tell you to take your stuff back. I'll buy the bar from you with my own money. But the rest, take back. I don't want it."

She turned the door handle, and Grant leaped out of his seat and charged the door, shutting it with his hand before she could open it.

"You're right," he whispered. "I handled this all wrong."

She looked up at him. "What were you so afraid would happen if you let me in entirely?" she asked.

The truth rocked him harder than the damn plane he'd taken at the start of all this.

"I was afraid that I'd lose you."

"Well, you lost me anyway, genius," she said quickly.

A small grin tugged his lips. "But I plan on getting you back."

"And how do you plan that?" she asked.

"Well, since this is my company, and we set into motion new rules that I can't be voted out, Laythem Inc. is secure, and I can telecommute. Say, from . . . Oregon."

Her lips parted, and her eyes widened. "You'd really come to live in Yachats?"

"I would do anything for you," he said. Cupping her face, he urged her gaze to stay locked on his. "I'm sorry I went about that in the wrong way."

He'd wanted to hold on to his father's company and memory, yet he was doing both a disservice by turning from the real-life woman who made him a better man.

She smiled, and he caught a single tear running down her face with his thumb.

"I love you, Hannah."

"I love you, too," she breathed, and he kissed her hard. With everything he was feeling, everything he missed, everything he had, he kissed his wife.

Because she was finally in his arms, and there was no amount of money or distance that would ever keep him from her again.

"Well, since I'm here in New York," she said against his mouth, "I suppose I could spend a few days with you before we get back to Yachats. Maybe take you out to dinner. Apparently I'm a millionaire now."

He smiled. "The sexiest millionaire in the world."

"I think you have me beat on that one," she said and melted into him, her soft lips parting to drink him in, and Grant fell hopelessly for the love of his life. His wife. Again.

Epilogue

Hannah wiped down the counter at Goonies and looked around. She smiled at the upgrades and remodel Cal had done over the past few months.

The bar was busy, and Hannah was happy.

Beyond happy.

She had a little house, a little bar, and a very large man. All of which she loved. The latter more than the others. The only bummer was that it wasn't her neck that was hurting anymore. It was her lower back. But that was to be expected when—

"Hannah, can I get another drink here?" Larry yelled at her, interrupting her daydreaming.

She huffed at Larry and poured him another round. His white beard was getting longer and scragglier. "Seriously, how are you not in the morgue yet?"

"You should be nicer to your best customer," the old man grumbled, and Hannah placed a bowl of peanuts in front of him. He had a point. The man did drink here a lot.

"You should try an iced tea and a salad sometime. Good for your health. Some people may want you around for a while longer yet," she said and patted the top of his hand.

He laughed. "Ah, no one wants me around that long."

Hannah shot him a smile and walked down the bar. Her feet were killing her. She had hired two bartenders so that she didn't have to work all the time. Business was booming, Grant was due back from New York tonight, and she was so excited to see him that nothing could bring her mood down.

She looked at the clock. Five more hours, then Grant would land and finally be on his way home.

The door opened, and she prepared herself for another customer . . . but it wasn't a customer who walked through the door.

"I hear this is the best bar in town, where the most gorgeous woman in the world works," Grant said, walking through the entrance in his three-piece suit. He looked like he'd just come straight out of the pages of *GQ*.

"Grant!" She ran around the bar and straight at him, throwing herself into his arms. He wrapped her up, her feet lifting off the floor as he kissed her.

"I missed you so much," he said and kissed her neck, her eyelids, her nose.

"You were only gone a week," she said.

"Don't remind me. You need to come with me next time. I can't be away from you that long." He kissed her again.

"Well, I don't think I can," she said, and he leaned back, setting her down on her feet.

"Why?"

She shrugged. "I'm just not sure if I'm allowed to fly during my first trimester."

"What does that—" Grant cut off his own words, and his dark eyes shot wide. "Are you . . ." He placed a hand on her stomach.

She nodded and smiled. "You're going to be a daddy."

A bright white smile took up his whole face, and he hugged her again, kissing her like crazy all over her mouth.

"And you're going to be the best mother in the world." He cupped her face and kissed her hard. "My baby's having my baby!" he yelled out, and the entire bar cheered.

Then Larry hollered, "Yeah, just watch out for those mood swings. Especially from Hannah—good luck to you, mister."

Hannah laughed. Grant didn't.

"Oh, shit, he's got a point," Grant said, looking down with a playful tease in his eyes. "You're stubborn and feisty without extra hormones . . ."

"Better watch your back, then, Laythem, because I'm coming for you."

He kissed her softly on the lips. "I wouldn't have it any other way. I'm at your service."

"Well, that's good, because I need your help with something," she whispered against his mouth.

"Anything."

"I need you to take me home and remind me why I miss you so much."

He grinned and smacked her butt.

"Done!"

Acknowledgments

Thank you, Lauren, for the wonderful edits; I enjoy working with you so much! Thank you, Jen and Jessica and the entire Montlake team. Thank you, Jill, for being a great agent.

About the Author

National and international bestselling author Joya Ryan is the author of more than a dozen adult and new-adult romance novels. Passionate about both cooking and dancing (despite not being too skilled at the latter), she loves traveling and seeking out new adventures. Visit her online at www.joyaryan.com.